FATED MAGIC

CLAIMED BY WOLVES #1

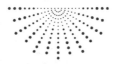

CALLIE ROSE

For updates on my upcoming releases and promotions, sign up for my
reader newsletter! I promise not to bite (or spam you).

CALLIE ROSE NEWSLETTER

SABLE

THE FLUORESCENT LIGHTS in the ceiling emit a faint, incessant buzzing that hurts my battered head almost as much as the harsh illumination does. I stare down at Doctor Patil's shiny black hair as his capable fingers, clad in sapphire blue surgical gloves, prod at my ankle.

He's already shined his light in my eyes and checked my pupils for signs of concussion. He declared me safe from brain damage, but he let out a long, low whistle at the other parts of me that weren't so lucky.

The doctor presses on a particularly sore spot, and I hiss through my teeth, gripping the paper-covered table beneath me.

"This area hurts?" Doctor Patil asks, pressing the nodule again like a damn sadist.

My jaw tightens as I try to restrain the impulse to yank my leg out of his grasp. "Yes. That area hurts."

I notice his gaze pause over the crescent-shaped scars above my knee, but he doesn't say anything. The same suspicious look crossed his face when he saw the scars on my arms. And again when he lifted my shirt to press on my stomach to check for any internal abnormalities, only to find more scars—some of them old and faded, some a fresh, shiny pink.

Doctor Patil steps back and settles onto his little rolling stool. Scooting away from me a little, he dips his head to catch my gaze, his words measured and careful. "Tell me again how it happened. Can you do that, Sable?"

Uncle Clint shifts, the movement so minute that I bet the doctor doesn't even notice. My uncle is standing against the wall by the door with his blue flannel shirt tucked into his Wranglers, the sleeves rolled to his elbows. He has the darkly tanned skin of a man who's spent his life beneath the Montana sun—and that particular planetary body has done little to preserve any of the good looks he might have once had. Now, north of fifty with a balding head, he looks like a dried, wrinkled potato with a beer belly.

He glares at me over Doctor Patil's head, dark eyes promising retribution if I so much as put a toe out of line.

My stomach seems to turn in on itself, an all-too-familiar heaviness settling over me as I look back at the doctor.

"I fell," I say around the lump in my throat. "Down the stairs. Carrying the laundry to the basement."

"Are you often clumsy?" Doctor Patil glances down at my chart then back up at me. He has startling gray eyes that seem to be at odds with his dark skin and hair. They also seem to *see* a lot more than my usual doctor.

I shrug, goosebumps breaking out on my skin as my nerves prickle. The ruthless fluorescents shine too much light on the scars that cover my body. Each thin line of knotted white skin tells a story that my uncle doesn't want told. After years of visits, years of injuries and bruises and strange ailments, Doctor Jones only sees the dollar signs each of those things ticks off on his final bill. He doesn't ask questions. But Doctor Jones is out this week, so we got Doctor Patil instead.

Uncle Clint doesn't bring me to the hospital for every little injury. Only the bad ones, the ones that clearly need extra care. Unfortunately for him, he pushed me too hard tonight.

And unfortunately for us both, Doctor Patil asks questions.

"I have an inner ear abnormality," I say, parroting the same excuse I've used for years. "My balance is awful. Uncle Clint tells me to use the laundry chute, but I'm stubborn."

I smile, trying to add a bit of warmth behind my last

statement, but I'm absolutely certain it looks more pained than affectionate.

Doctor Patil narrows his eyes, then swivels on his stool. "Mr. Maddock? Could you give me and Sable a moment alone?"

Uncle Clint straightens up from the wall but leaves his arms crossed over his barrel chest. "No, sir. You ain't our usual doctor. I won't be leaving my precious girl alone with no stranger."

God, Doctor Patil would have to be a moron to not hear the syrupy false note in my uncle's voice.

Precious girl. Right. More like *punching bag.*

Doctor Patil, to his credit, doesn't seem the least bit intimidated by Clint's brutish warning. "You understand that at eighteen years old, she's a grown adult, and she would be well within her right to ask you to leave the room."

My skin goes cold as I understand what he's telling me. *Say the word, Sable, and I'll have security remove him from the room so we can really chat.* His clipped Indian accent and his deep, melodious voice is a balm to all the aches I've ever walked into this building with—even the ones on the inside.

But I can't do what he's suggesting. I can't tell Uncle Clint to leave so that I can confide in this sweet doctor who *knows* something isn't right.

"No, that's okay. I'd prefer that my uncle stay with

me." My voice comes out small. Dejected. I'm sure Doctor Patil can hear that too. Clint and I are putting on a soap opera, and this man sees right through it. Too bad there's not a damn thing he can do to save me.

Doctor Patil swivels on his stool again, his long white coat swishing. He purses his lips as he looks at me, like he's trying to solve a puzzle that's missing key pieces. There's pity in his gaze, concern etched into the lines that frame his mouth.

"Sable, are you okay?" He speaks slowly, as if willing me to answer with the truth.

Uncle Clint's gaze is like fire searing my face, and my stomach twists into an even tighter knot.

"Well, doc, I fell down the stairs and broke my arm, so I'd say I've had better days," I joke, forcing levity into my tone. I want to signal to this man—this *good* man—that I need help. I want to admit to him that my uncle beats me and keeps me locked up in the house like an animal.

But I can't. I know too well what will happen to me if I even hint at the truth.

I plaster a smile on my face. "Other than the bumps and bruises, I'm fine."

Doctor Patil gives me a hard look. Acid burns up my throat as nausea bubbles up inside me. I pray that he'll give up. The harder he fights to get the truth out of me, the worse it will be for me later. *Please, please let it go,* I urge him silently, keeping that damn lunatic smile on my face.

"Excuse me. Doctor?"

We're interrupted by the nurse arriving with my x-rays, and my muscles unclench a little as Doctor Patil stands to take them from her. Uncle Clint keeps his glare on me as the doctor strides to the viewing box and shoves them into place, hitting a switch to illuminate the images.

My arm fills the white screen. I remember reading once that there are sixty-four bones in the arm, and they're all just right there on display. A bunch of shades of gray that make up my insides. I wonder if Doctor Patil can see the bones that have been broken before.

Do they grow back harder? More crooked? Like my heart does?

"Ah. Well. Good news, Sable." Doctor Patil turns around, shoving his hands into the deep pockets of his coat. "No broken bones after all. I'd venture to guess we've got a sprained wrist, like I suggested before."

My smile turns a bit more genuine at that news. I wasn't looking forward to healing another broken bone. Not that sprained wrists hurt any less, but the downtime for fractures is hell. Plus, my bones have been through enough over the years. I consider this a win.

Doctor Patil finishes up, equipping me with a wrist brace and instructions to give it a rest for the next few weeks. He tells me to rest my ankle too, if possible, and I nod dutifully at his instructions.

And that's it.

He can't do anything for all the bruises, and he can't do anything to save me from a situation he knows in his gut is wrong, so when all is said and done, he sends me on my way.

This is how it will always be. The words slip through my mind like poison as I walk away from Doctor Patil's kind, concerned gaze. *I'll always live in fear. I'll always be a prisoner. And no one can help me.*

Fear follows me through the maze of hallways as I walk through the medical center in Uncle Clint's shadow. He grips the keys to his Silverado as if they're a weapon and anyone who stands in his way might get a key to the eye. There's mud on his boots, and he leaves a trail of dried flakes on the clean hospital floor.

Electric doors slide open with a *whoosh* before we step out into the dry, cool evening air. Night fell sometime while Doctor Patil was trying to save my life, and I close my eyes, breathing in the scent of pine and distant snow. The hospital Clint took me to is a good twenty miles away from our small town, but no matter where I go, I can always smell the mountains. The mountains steady me. They stand over my little piece of Montana like sentinels in the distance, proof that the wind can scream and storms can rage, but they will never bend.

The alarm chirps on Uncle Clint's maroon Chevy Silverado. He's already in the cab behind the wheel by the time I manage to haul myself into the passenger seat. My limbs are ready to give in, my body ready to crumple into a ball and sleep. Climbing into his ridiculously jacked up truck hurts almost as much as the fall did.

He jams his key in the ignition and turns on the car. Classic country blares from the speakers, and Uncle Clint turns the music down enough for me to hear him say, "You did good, girl."

My stomach turns. I don't respond, turning away from him and tucking myself against the passenger side door to put as much distance between us as possible.

I stay that way as he turns the music back up and begins to drive. It's back roads all the way home, twenty miles but thirty minutes accounting for stop signs and wildlife. Neither of us speak, but I can't get Doctor Patil's knowing gray eyes out of my head. I keep going over the entire visit with a fine-toothed comb, wondering if I could have done something differently this time.

If I'd been braver or smarter, maybe I could have ended this nightmare. Instead, I'm barreling back toward my prison without an end in sight.

Hot tears prick my eyes.

Dammit. I hate feeling so fucking helpless.

I'm watching the trees pass like ghosts in the darkness along the side of the road when my uncle suddenly slams on the brakes. The truck's tires lock up as it skids to a stop, the lighter bed fishtailing sideways so that we come to a rest across both lanes of the empty road.

A deer is standing outside the arc of the headlights. The angle we've come to rest at puts him just beyond my door. He's massive, all muscle and antlers, more regal than anything I've ever seen. His eyes glint in the moonlight as he stares at the truck, still as a statue.

Then he turns and bolts off into the night.

"Son of a fucking bitch!" Uncle Clint roars, slamming a hand to the steering wheel. "These goddamn deer! Almost ruined my fucking truck."

His blow and raised voice send terror shooting through me, and I press closer to the door, making as much space between us as I can.

My uncle grumbles something else about his precious Silverado, but I don't hear him. Adrenaline rushes through my veins as I watch the deer disappear into the trees, and a strange feeling washes over me.

Mr. Maddock? Could you give me and Sable a moment alone?

He tried to help me.

Doctor Patil tried to help, and I didn't even take the *chance* that he might be able to.

When will my next chance be? How many more chances will I get before my uncle kills me?

I'm eighteen. What will my life look like when I'm twenty? Twenty-five?

Uncle Clint will never let me go. He hates me too

much, and he's too fucking sadistic to ever let me leave his house in one piece.

But I'm not in his house right now.

In this moment, the only thing standing between me and freedom is this car door.

A wave of absolute clarity washes over me, making all the blood in my body turn to ice. *It's now or never.*

So I throw myself out the door and take my chance, sprinting off after the deer.

2

SABLE

I sprint like I don't have a twisted ankle and a sprained wrist. I sprint like I'm not covered in painful bruises with the energy level of a factory in nuclear meltdown. Because this is it—this is my only chance to get away from him once and for all, and I will *not* fail.

Because if I do, he'll kill me. I know that with dead certainty.

Uncle Clint shouts, his snarl a whip cracking after me. I can't make out his words through the adrenaline rushing in my ears, and honestly, I don't even want to try. The coward I was before would have frozen at that tone. I would have turned around and returned to him with my tail between my legs, closing my eyes against whatever punishment he deemed fit.

But I'm not that girl. I refuse to continue to be *that girl* anymore. I stopped being her the second I opened that car door.

Doctor Patil tried to save me. He wanted to give me the out I needed, and I didn't take him up on his offer.

So it's up to me now.

Uncle Clint will chase me. But I'm smaller, quicker, lighter. And my life depends on this. I'll run until my legs collapse before I let him catch up to me.

The sound of the deer leaping ahead of me is like a beacon in the pitch dark night. I follow that sound beyond the flat plain and into the woods, giving myself over to the wilderness. Uncle Clint's curses follow me, but they grow weaker as I fly over the thick undergrowth.

My ankle should hurt. I think it *does* hurt, but there's too much adrenaline and panic flooding my body for me to feel anything but the desperate burn in my lungs.

Low-hanging branches slap at my arms and face, and I know they're leaving more marks on my body to add to the ones I already have, but I don't care. I keep moving, focusing on the sharp inhalations and exhalations of my breath, because if I stop to think, my throbbing injuries will overtake me. I can't afford to stumble.

Not now. Not so close to freedom.

Before long, my uncle's string of obscenities peters out. The man's out of shape and has no business running through the woods. His heavy footfalls fade little by little, until I can't hear him anymore at all.

A giddy laugh escapes my lips, disappearing into the broad expanse of woods around me.

Jesus. Am I doing this? Really?

My old terror rises when I realize I've reached the point of no return. If he finds me now, I'll pay for it in ways I can't even imagine. I've just done the most terrifying thing I could possibly do—run from my abuser. And if he finds me now, he'll beat me until I can't run anymore.

Or worse, until I'm dead.

I can never go back.

A fresh surge of adrenaline pours through me, and I put on another burst of speed. I've lost track of the deer, which isn't too surprising. There's no way I could run as fast as the buck, and I don't know the landscape of the forest like he does. But I'm thankful he was there for a short time and helped give me the clarity I needed to run.

The deer was another Doctor Patil. Another sign from the universe. He saved my life by doing what he does best, and showing me that I could too.

Even though I can no longer hear Uncle Clint pursuing me, I'm not dumb enough to think he's given up. It's likely he's hurrying back to his pickup, where he'll slam into the driver's seat and take off to look for me. As long as I stay in the woods and far away from the roads, I should be safe.

But as soon as I have the thought, the woods begin to thin out. I spill onto the narrow shoulder of a road, my sneakers slapping on pavement before I even realize what's happened. In the same instant that I recognize the yellow lines beneath my feet, headlights flash over me.

I freeze, panic turning me to stone.

The car bearing down on me is nothing but two bright circles of light as its headlights blind me. My mind screams at me to run, to leap off the road, to get out of the way. *What if it's Uncle Clint?*

But fear has rendered me incapable of even lifting a finger or turning away so I don't have to see my death coming.

An ungodly screech emits from beneath the car, and it slings sideways. Not an accidental save this time thanks to a light rear end, as it was for Uncle Clint. A defense maneuver. I have a brief moment to think, *Oh, thank God, it's not a truck,* before I realize the car is still coming toward me, skidding sideways as momentum drags it across the pavement.

As if I could somehow stop a moving vehicle, I throw my hands out. The car screeches a moment longer and then halts. My palms slap uselessly against the door, and pain shoots up my injured wrist.

But I'm alive.

My heart is somewhere beneath the car, still fluttering like a terrified bird. I lock gazes with the driver, struck dumb by the fact I almost just died—that I finally made a break for my freedom and nearly lost my life before I could even complete my escape.

The man is... beautiful. Almost inhumanly so. Sharp features, strong jaw, messy black hair, and a five o'clock shadow that's seen the darker side of midnight.

He looks like some kind of ancient god who rose up out of the darkness and will return there as soon as I blink.

We're frozen, both of us, gaping at each other for several long seconds as if time has stopped.

I'm not sure who moves first, but in the same instant that he reaches for his seatbelt, I take off toward the other side of the road and the shelter of the woods. My ankle throbs as I crash through the undergrowth and dart around trees.

But I don't stop.

I run and run, until all hint of civilization is far behind me, until I'm crossing shallow streams instead of roads, until I'm climbing steeply pitched slopes into the foothills. I lose all sense of time and direction. I could be racing headlong into the pits of hell, and I wouldn't care—I'll keep going until Clint can't find me, even if the devil can.

The moon is high, a sliver of light barely breaking through the canopy overhead when I pause and lean against a thick tree trunk to catch my breath. My chest burns as if my lungs are on fire, and my muscles are shaky and weak. I lean over, pressing my hands into my knees, and focus on taking deep breaths. As the adrenaline wears off and the sharp pain of each breath begins to fade, heat rises in my injured ankle. I've probably turned the "twist" into a sprain.

Great, I think, straightening and laying my head back against the cool bark. *A sprained ankle to match my sprained wrist. I'm stylish as fuck.*

I almost laugh again into the darkness, and I have a fleeting worry that I'm losing my mind. I don't feel like... myself.

My life has been an unending monotony of boredom, fear, and pain for so long that the number of new things that've happened tonight leaves me reeling. My mind can't quite comprehend all of it, and when I try to comprehend the enormity of what I've done, something powerful and overwhelming rises up in my chest.

If I let that thing grow too big, I know it will crush me. It will dwarf me, leaving me curled up in a ball on the ground.

So I push thoughts of any future beyond the next few minutes away. That's all I can handle right now. A minute at a time.

Pressing a hand to the lingering stitch in my side, I scan the dark forest around me.

I'm not sure what my plan is from here, but I don't want to stay still for too long. I know chances are slim Uncle Clint will find me this deep in the wilderness, but why tempt fate? I can find somewhere to shelter overnight—a cave, or a tree, maybe, so I don't get eaten by bears.

As I shove away from the tree to get moving, a wave of dizziness crashes over me. I stumble, catching myself against the trunk before I can keel over into the undergrowth. The run took a lot out of me. More than I realized, which is stupid really, considering I'm fresh off a hospital visit.

I lift my head, focusing on the tree as I try to blink away the fog that clouds my vision. There are strange dark lines etched into the bark beneath my palm, and I lift my hand, swaying as I let all my weight settle back on my legs. The trunk is marked with some kind of odd pattern.

Bears, I think, scraping my fingertips down the claw marks. *It's just bears.* Not that the idea of bears being nearby gave me any kind of comfort. And what kind of bears make marks that look so stylized?

My feet are infinitely heavy as I turn and stumble away from the marked-up tree. I couldn't run now if I tried, but I keep my pace as quick as I can. I trip over my own feet several times, barely able to stay upright, but I manage to move several more yards through the trees. Those strange marks are on a bunch of these trunks, but I'm too tired and strung out to wonder what they are anymore.

The farther I walk, the more my vision tunnels and the woozier I feel. When the ground ahead of me dips downward sharply, I'm not prepared for it. My steps falter, and I stumble, falling forward. I flail, arms thrashing out to my sides for anything I can grab to keep me from hitting the ground.

But the trees have grown farther apart, and I have nothing to hold on to.

I tumble down the side of a ravine, a pained grunt forcing its way out of my lungs as my body rolls over the rough rocks and dirt.

When I come to a stop at the bottom of the ravine, darkness overtakes me.

IT'S STILL DARK when my eyes open again.

My mind is only half-alert, and I have no idea how much time has passed since I blacked out. It could have been minutes or maybe hours.

I can't seem to move my limbs. I'm on my stomach, my cheek pressed into the dry dirt and my arms tangled beneath me. It's colder here, and my extremities ache from the chill. My blonde hair is draped over my face, partially obscuring my vision.

But I can see enough to know that I'm not alone.

A shadow prowls toward me on four paws, a glistening snout sniffing at the air. Not a bear, as I expected, but a wolf. It takes a few tentative steps toward me, its giant paws silent on the ground.

Fear prickles at the edges of my consciousness. I'm too hurt, too exhausted to move. I can't even seem to get an open line of communication between my brain and my arms, even with the fight-or-flight response currently pumping through my body.

So I just close my eyes and hope death comes quickly.

I MUST HAVE PASSED out again.

In my next brief moment of consciousness, which is barely more than a flicker of awareness, I feel strong, warm arms slide around my broken body.

Then I'm lifted, and we're moving, my head resting against a broad chest and a stranger's heartbeat.

3

RIDGE

WHEN I LEFT the cabin and shifted into wolf form to patrol the borders of my pack's land, I had no idea my trip back home would include carrying a beautiful, unconscious woman against my naked body.

Granted, most men wouldn't hate this particular situation. The girl is stunning, even with all the cuts and bruises. Golden hair that falls in a thick curtain around her shoulders. Petite, but with perfect curves beneath her tight blue jeans and gray sweatshirt. The kind of heart-shaped face poets dedicate entire stanzas to in the throes of their passion.

But this sure as shit wasn't how I expected to spend my night. Not to mention, I feel like a fucking perv holding her while my cock dangles freely beneath her ass. Shifting into a wolf is great as long as you don't need clothes when you shift back.

Still barely conscious, the girl moves restlessly in my arms, wincing as she draws her injured wrist to her chest. The limb is wrapped in a hard brace, which I take to mean it was hurt *before* she took a tumble down Devil's Ditch and landed at my pack's doorstep.

Something that tastes a lot like pity wells up inside me as I glance down at her sleeping face. She looks like a princess in the moonlight, small and fragile and beat all to hell. She deserves a white knight to carry her off into the sunrise on his noble steed.

Instead, she got the fucking big bad wolf.

What the fuck was she doing all the way out here? Devil's Ditch isn't even accessible by road. It's miles from any civilization that doesn't belong to my pack. Humans can't just stumble onto our land like they're out for a hike in the national park or some shit. We've made sure of that.

Jesus, she's lucky I even found her.

I almost took a different route tonight. The protected boundary stretches atop the cliff, and I came out this way prepared to climb up and check on our sigils to make sure they were still firmly intact. Some vague instinct kept me from climbing to the top of the cliff—wolf's intuition or some shit—and coaxed me into the ravine instead. If not for that, the girl might have laid out there and died as the temperature dropped overnight, then became vulture food tomorrow morning.

Unfortunately, her presence means my patrol got cut off early. Not a good night for a distraction.

We've heard rumors of dark witch activity scented in the area, which is exactly why I wanted to check out the boundaries to begin with. Typically, where we smell a witch, there's a witch to be found, and having to lug this injured lamb back to my cabin is gonna keep me from doing my duties as alpha. My pack's protection comes first and foremost.

It's supposed to, anyway.

So why the actual fuck am I carrying this chick back to my cabin? Why do I even care that she looks like she's been torn to pieces and tossed out like trash? She's not a shifter, and she's not my responsibility. I should drop her in a soft spot away from anywhere she could be exposed to danger and leave her there. Not my problem.

And yet... I won't.

For one thing, I'm not that fucking heartless. She's young and fragile-looking, and I guarantee she wouldn't know how to survive out here even in broad daylight. I'm not a monster, even on days when I feel like I am.

So I readjust her weight in my arms and press on.

I keep my steps light as I stride into the quiet village my pack has built for itself. Most of us are night owls, but it's late even for wolves, so the majority of the pack is sleeping. We're sometime in the darkness before dawn is my best guess. I was on foot for a couple hours before I came across the girl, and I started my patrol pretty late.

Moving quickly and silently, I make my way through the small village. My gaze roams the shadows surrounding my pack members' homes, searching for any sign of life. Nobody here would be happy that I've brought an outsider in. Sure, I could growl and grunt and pull rank, but the path of least resistance seems best in the current moment.

And that path is stealth.

I'll get her cleaned up, wait for her to wake up and figure out her story, then decide what happens from there. Maybe she just needs a ride somewhere. Maybe she was taking a hike and lost her way. Wouldn't be the first time some idiot hiker nearly died in the wilderness for biting off more than they could chew.

I shift her weight into one arm so I can open the door to my cabin. My hand is dangerously close to the girl's nicely rounded ass, and a tingle of warmth shoots through me. I rein in the beast with a stern, *for fuck's sake, man, she's unconscious and beaten,* and shove the door open with my bare foot.

The house still smells like the dinner I cooked earlier, a medley of lamb and rosemary. I add the scent of her body to the mix—the thick, cloying smell of dirt, the tang of a mountain stream, and something a little more feminine underneath it all. Flowery.

This cabin isn't acquainted with flowery.

I carry her to my bedroom and gently lay her on top of the covers. She's soaked through, which is the source of the mountain stream smell, I'm sure. I peel off her torn, filthy sweatshirt and discard it on the floor, then reach for the button on her jeans. I'm trying desperately not to notice the perfect mounds of flesh cupped by a delicate pink bra, but it's hard not to.

Studiously avoiding her tits, I tug on the waistband of her jeans, struggling to get them over her ass. When they finally begin to peel away, they expose a pair of soft cotton panties. They're not anything special, not fancy lingerie made of lace, but my heart skips a damn beat at the way they hug the curves of her hip bones.

Jesus fucking Christ. Gritting my teeth, I avert my eyes and head for the closet. I need to cover her, and even more than that, I need to cover *me*.

How did I end up in this situation?

I yank on a pair of sweatpants and a t-shirt, then find an old, worn pair of pajama pants that might not fall off her gorgeous ass. They'll have to be rolled eighty times to keep from tripping her up, but they'll do.

I toss the pants over her hips, hiding those infernal panties so that I can take stock of the situation without distraction, and lean over her, running my gaze over her wounds. Whatever she did, she got torn up anywhere she had bare skin—the kinds of small scratches that might come from sharp tree limbs and a full speed chase.

24

But the scratches aren't the only thing I notice, and my eyes narrow as my gaze moves over her small form.

The girl's covered in scars.

They're everywhere. On her smooth, pale abdomen. Above her round breasts, across her clavicle. Down her arms, her legs, even her fucking feet. Small scars, round scars, cuts so thin they look like they were carved intentionally. Some old, some new, and some nearly as fresh as the wrist brace on her arm. The worst of them appear to be situated on parts of her body easily hidden by clothes.

As if they were put on her intentionally.

Pure rage envelops me, and I grip the t-shirt I'm holding so hard I feel my nails dig into my palms through the fabric. She's so fucking beautiful. So fragile, breakable, soft... Who would hurt this woman? How could they live with themselves?

I'm surprised by the intensity of my anger. Uncurling my fingers from the t-shirt, I breathe through the fury as I gently tug the shirt over her head.

With the most intimate of her injuries covered, I feel a little more level-headed. I move on to the pants, pulling them up over her hips and keeping my eyes firmly on her sleeping face instead of the panties.

Then I roll her gently beneath the covers, pulling them up over her shoulders. She turns over in her sleep, curling into a fetal position beneath my quilt, her hands tucked beneath her cheek. I tuck the blankets gently around her, marveling again at how lovely she is. Despite the fact that my cock has a mind of its own and she's got a body like a goddess, this isn't the kind of girl you fuck and run. I can smell the innocence on her; smell the goodness in her.

Moving to the door, I extinguish the bedroom light and leave her to her rest.

As far as I'm concerned, no one will hurt this girl again.

I'll make damn fucking sure of it.

4

SABLE

I wake up slowly, as if my body and mind are resisting consciousness. My dreams were surprisingly calm and comforting, and my eyes don't seem to want to open. I don't want to leave this calm, peaceful space between sleep and waking.

And why would I? So much of my life has been pain and trauma that it's only fair I linger in the good moments as long as I can.

I'm beneath soft, warm blankets in a quiet room, and for a moment, I think I'm back in my bed in Uncle Clint's house. But then a comforting scent wafts over me. Not the usual smell of Tide and my lavender body lotion.

Something more masculine.

Woodsy and spicy.

Unfamiliar yet achingly intoxicating.

I nestle farther into the pillow, breathing the soothing

scent in deeply. I slide beneath the covers, ignoring the pained protests of my body as I roll into the sheets and take another deep breath. I spread out on my belly, blankets covering me from head to toe, and smile as I'm completely surrounded by this woodsy smell. Even still, I want more of it.

I'm rubbing against the sheets like a cat, like I can imprint myself with the smell, when the events of last night suddenly rush back into my memories with a vengeance.

My heart seizes in my chest as I freeze, my breath catching.

The hospital visit.

The drive home.

I... I *ran*.

I remember shoving open the truck door and racing off into the woods to the sound of Uncle Clint spitting mad and making chase. There was a deer leading me, and I was almost hit by a car. Were there... bear claw marks on trees? I fell down a ravine...

And then there was a wolf.

Everything after that is a dark, unformed blur. But what I *do* remember is enough to send panic spiking through my veins.

Shoving back the covers, I sit up in bed and glance frantically around the room. Four unfamiliar walls surround me, constructed of wooden logs like some kind of rustic cabin. There's nothing in the room but a bed and a dresser, and two doors, both closed. A small window is set into an exterior wall, covered by gauzy white curtains that let in golden sunlight—*afternoon* sunlight, maybe.

Shit. How long was I asleep?

Then my gaze lands on a pile of dirty laundry resting in a basket in one corner. Men's blue jeans, white t-shirts...

I slide from the bed, staring at the pile as I move across the room toward it.

Right on top of the laundry is a blue flannel shirt.

No.

I stumble backward, arms wheeling as I put too much weight on my sore ankle and lose my balance. My hip crash-lands on the bed, and the frame scrapes across the floor. I cringe at how loud the sound is, gripping the baseboard in total silence as I brace myself for someone to come running.

Somewhere out in the house, a floorboard creaks, and my heart leaps into a gallop.

Shit. Shitshitshit.

My uncle must have found me before the wolf could eat me. And now Clint has dragged me to some cabin in the woods, somewhere nobody will hear me scream. He's been waiting for me to wake up so he can punish me.

So he can teach me a lesson for trying to run away.

He'll kill me this time. I just know it.

I leap to my feet and race toward the window, shoving

aside the curtains. For a terrifying minute, I think the damn thing is nailed shut, until I realize there's a safety catch on the rail that I have to unlatch in order to raise it. Footsteps are moving through the house beyond the closed door, coming closer. Uncle Clint isn't hurried, obviously. He probably thinks I'm too injured to get away, especially after finding me at the bottom of a ravine.

Jesus, I'm lucky to be alive.

The fleeting thought flits through my mind a second before something falls to the floor in the other room with a jarring clang.

My luck is about to run out.

Every single thud of those unhurried steps makes my hands shake harder. It's difficult enough trying to maneuver my fingers above the wrist brace with pain lancing up my arm, but the adrenaline pumping through me makes my hands shake so badly that it's almost impossible. I finally manage to slide my thumb up with enough force to unlock the catch, then lean my shoulder in and jam the window open.

Cool mountain air gusts into the room, tickling my skin, and I take a deep breath of the familiar scent of distant snow and evergreens, hoping it will calm me.

It doesn't fucking work, but it hardly matters. The footsteps outside the room are almost here, and I'm running on pure self-preservation instinct now, an almost animalistic drive to just fucking *survive*.

The window isn't set high on the wall, thank God, so I don't have to haul myself up to get through it. As soon as it's open wide enough, I've got my torso out the window, sliding to freedom on my belly with all the elegance of a hippo on a dry water slide.

I land awkwardly on the ground outside, landing on my arms and shoulders. My legs flop out after me, the momentum sending me into a graceless barrel roll.

With a soft grunt, I come to rest on my side. The strange, oversized pajama pants I'm wearing have unfolded at the bottoms. They're too long—a man's pair of thin flannels that trail a foot past my feet. I consider rolling them back up and hoping they'll stay in place, but the reality is, they're loose and thin and I'm out of time. So I shove the damn things down my legs and kick them off.

My body protests as I use the thick logs on the outside of the cabin to pull myself to my feet. I can put weight on my twisted ankle, thankfully, but it hurts like hell. I know my race through the woods last night didn't help the situation, but it's not like I had a choice then, any more than I have a choice now.

I have to get the hell out of here.

Fight, Sable. Run. Stay alive.

I shove away from the cabin, taking a few tentative steps to make sure my legs aren't going to collapse beneath me. Then I break into a run, trying not to think about the fact that my ass is on display for God and everyone to see.

At least the large t-shirt hangs down low enough to cover most of it.

There are other cabins nearby, but I don't dare knock on any of their doors begging for help. Clint's good at making friends, and I can't count on any strangers taking my side over his.

The tree line of a thick forest is only a hundred yards away to my left, and I run in that direction, hoping to get lost in the trees like I did last night. The memory of my dark flight to freedom sends a surge of anger and frustration through me that I channel into my legs.

I can't believe Clint found me. I must've run miles into deep wilderness, through woods and up into the foothills. He never allowed me to have a cell phone; hell, I couldn't even wear a watch under his rules.

So did he have some kind of tracker implanted in me like a psychopath?

Sadly, I wouldn't put something like that past him. I wouldn't put anything past him, and I'm reminded starkly of how foolish my unplanned flight was.

I didn't think through any of this. I just ran.

And now I have no choice but to keep running.

There's a rough dirt road beneath my bare feet—dry, dusty ground that hasn't seen a good rainfall in a few days. I know that probably means I'm leaving a billowing trail of dust in my wake, but either side of the road is lined by small, rustic houses, so there's no other route I can take.

My arms and legs pump harder as I go for a bit more speed.

I don't recognize this place. It's not Big Creek, the town where I lived with Uncle Clint—at least, I don't think it is. I wasn't exactly allowed out of the house to get to know the area, but we drove through it every time we made the trip to the hospital or the few other errands he took me on. I don't recall a distinct lack of power lines, and we definitely drove on asphalt roads, not dirt and gravel.

Out of the corner of my eye, I catch sight of a few people. But I don't let myself look for more than a second, keeping my head down and praying none of them sound the alarm.

If Uncle Clint brought me to this place, it means he has friends here. Friends who don't care what he gets up to in his own home, or how he abuses his niece. I can't trust any of these people to help me. I couldn't before, and I definitely can't now that I've run away.

The full force of his anger is about to come down on me like a hammer falling, unless I can get away a second time.

The dirt road ends abruptly at thick grass, and I cross the line with a surge of relief. I'm almost there. Grass is springier than the packed dirt road, and I use it to my advantage, running faster, my breaths coming quicker.

Dear God, please just let me get away. Please give me a chance to live a better life.

The trees, and what little protection they might offer, are only a few feet away.

But before I can reach them, two arms wrap tightly around my waist, hauling me off the ground and pinning me against a solid chest.

5
RIDGE

GODDAMMIT. This isn't how I wanted to get a half-naked girl in my arms.

Normal guys, they go to parties. Go to bars. They talk up the first hot woman who shakes her ass in their direction, then fuck her senseless against a bathroom wall covered in graffiti that probably includes her phone number.

Not me. No, my dumb ass has to find an unconscious woman in the wilderness and bring her home, only for her to strip to her panties and race madly through the village in an attempt to escape.

I mean, I know I'm not *People*'s Sexiest Man Alive, but damn.

The girl's head slams back toward my face, and I have to crane my neck sideways to keep from getting a busted nose.

"Hey! I'm not going to hurt you!" I snarl as she tries again, whipping my head back the other way.

"Then put me down and let me go!" she gasps, struggling against my hold. She has a light, bell-like voice, though the bite to her statement takes some of the melody away. One bare foot catches me in the shin, and I grunt at the burst of pain. But so does she—hitting bones with bare limbs is like kicking concrete.

On the third attempted headbutt, I lack any other option. Locking one arm around her waist, I wrap her long hair around my other hand and tug her head back. Not enough to hurt her, but enough to pin her firmly in place against my body. In any other situation, I'd be following this move up with my lips on her earlobe, my tongue sliding down her neck. In this situation, that would be highly inappropriate.

But fuck if a part of me doesn't have a split second desire to do it.

"Calm down," I say softly in her ear as her torso pumps with hysterical breaths beneath my other arm. "You're hurt. You're going to make it worse."

Bad choice. That's when the screaming starts.

Jesus fucking Christ.

I thought I saved a sexy, blonde-haired princess last night, but this creature is a fucking banshee with the balls of a tiger. I knew the girl had been abused when I stripped her down and checked her injuries, but with her unconscious, I couldn't exactly ask after her mental state. It's clear now that I should have tied her to the bedposts for her own safety—and mine.

"Jesus, woman, I'm not going to hurt you!" I say, dragging her back the way we came. Dust is still settling on the road from our run through the village, but it's not enough cover to hide the spectacle she's making. Grady's over in his front yard, eyebrows chasing his receding hairline as he watches us with wide eyes. Cordelia Raney is sitting with her sister on the front porch, both of them staring at me like I'm killing the woman and dancing in her blood—though the two of them judge every fucking thing in sight, so I can't even care. Even more of my packmates are emerging from their houses to check out what's causing all the commotion.

Yeah. Not how I expected this day to go.

"Let me go!" The banshee punctuates the last word with a full body wave, clearly intending to slither out of my arms like a snake. But she has no idea I'm stronger than any man she's ever known, and she just jerks uselessly against my grasp. Unfortunately, that luscious ass I salivated over the night before slams right into my dick.

I pause and grit my teeth against the pain and nausea rolling through my insides from the blow. Damn it all to hell. We aren't even past the first row of houses, and she's still screaming.

Fuck. So much for keeping this quiet from the pack until I figure out what to do with her.

Since our current arrangement isn't going to work out —for her or my dick—I drop her to the ground. She's so startled, she immediately stops screaming. Gripping her waist, I whirl her around, catching sight of wide, tearful blue eyes that make a pit yawn open inside me. Then I lean over and jam my shoulder into her abdomen, hauling her up onto my shoulder.

Sometimes, you just gotta Neanderthal shit up.

I can move quicker now, ignoring the ever-growing curious stares from my pack as I head straight for my cabin. They aren't used to me having shit to do with women to begin with, and now they probably think I'm some kind of closet serial killer.

The girl's shock at being slung over my shoulder gives me a blessed moment of silence and stillness before she starts bucking like a fucking bronco and screaming like I'm ripping her skin off one strip at a time.

Shit. Putting her next to my head probably wasn't a great idea.

I lock my arm firmly around her thighs so that all she can move are her arms. It works—barely. I'll have some bruises and scratches on my back later, but if that's all I walk away from this alley cat with, I'll count myself fucking lucky.

Yanking open the screen door, I cross the threshold

into my cabin and then slam the front door behind me. I stop myself short of turning the lock.

Yeah, I don't want this mess of a woman launching headlong into the woods where another pack—or hell, one of those fucking witches—might not show her mercy. But I don't want her to think she's a prisoner either. I feel like I'm walking a tightrope, bringing a wild animal into my house and having to figure out the best way to navigate the situation.

Good thing I have experience with wild animals.

Sunlight spills through the large front window onto the smooth hardwood in my living room. I bend down, letting the woman flop out of my arms and onto the well-worn brown corduroy couch that's probably older than she is.

She's no longer screaming, not since we passed through the door into the house, but she's breathing like she just finished the Boston Marathon. Her fair skin looks even paler than it did in the dark of my bedroom last night, and with every breath she sucks in, she appears to have a harder time breathing.

Fuck. It hits me in a rush as I gaze at her. She's having a panic attack. I'm such an asshole.

I kneel on the ground before her and reach for her hands, being as gentle as possible. The girl's a deer, wide-eyed and terrified, and I'm the big bad wolf. I just have to convince her I'm not going to eat her.

She jolts away from me, but I manage to clasp her small hands. Her skin is soft and smooth.

"Hey. Hey, you're safe," I say, pitching my voice in the most soothing tone I can muster. Considering I have a deep baritone that sounds like I'm talking through gravel, it's a far reach for "soothing." I've got the kind of voice that leads a pack of feral wolves, not a namby-pamby motherly tone.

She sucks in breath after breath, but her fingers cling to mine. That's progress, right?

"I'm Ridge," I say when she doesn't reply. "You're in my cabin in the mountains. I found you last night. You were hurt, and I brought you home to take care of you. I'm not going to hurt you."

"H-how d-do I kn-know?" Every word comes out breathy, and on the heels of her statement, a crystalline tear crests over her lower eyelid and spills down her cheek.

My heart twinges in my chest. She's fucking terrified, so full of abject fear that she's desperate to escape. I can see in her gorgeous blue eyes that she fully expects I'm going to hurt her.

Just like the monster who marred her beautiful body.

"I can't prove it," I tell her truthfully, rubbing my thumbs over her fingers in what I hope is a calming gesture. "But I promise, I won't hurt you. I only want to help you."

We stare at one another for several moments. I keep rubbing the bend of her fingers and maintain a polite distance from her body so that I don't overstep and make her even more frightened than she already is. She's fucking beautiful, even with fear in her eyes and the pain etched on her face.

I want to destroy the person who turned her into this pitiful creature.

Finally, her shoulders slump forward, the tension in her body lessening by a fraction. She takes a deep, shaky breath and lets it out slowly.

I did it—I got through the panic.

"I'm sorry you woke up in a strange place. That was probably scary as fuck," I say, trying to get on her level, to show with my apology that I get it. "Especially after whatever happened to you last night. How'd you end up in Devil's Ditch? In the ravine?"

She blinks at me as if she's trying to relearn English. As if my words don't quite make sense, and she has to take an extra few seconds to sort through them as her brain comes back from whatever place it went to during her panic attack.

I don't move. Don't even blink. I just keep holding her hands, giving her the time and space she needs to answer.

Finally, her tongue darts out to lick her lips. She swallows once, then opens her mouth to speak.

But before she can say a word, several loud voices rise up outside the cabin. The girl's face changes instantly, and she recoils into the couch cushions, her gaze darting toward the front door.

I sigh, the sound a mixture of irritation and disgust. I recognize the voice clamoring loudest over the dull uproar.

The front door bangs open, and my brother, Lawson, barrels into the house as big as a mountain and wearing his fury like a cloak. A handful of his cronies rush in behind him, until my living room is nothing but pissed-off shifter energy.

"What the fuck, Ridge?" Lawson snarls, pointing at the girl.

Too late, I realize I should have locked that fucking door.

6

SABLE

For a moment, I got lost in Ridge's honey-colored eyes. I woke up expecting to come face-to-face with Uncle Clint, but what I ended up getting instead was pretty much the complete opposite of the man who raised me.

When the dark-haired man caught me near the trees, I was so certain I was about to die that I fought with everything I had in me. But inside his house, something shifted in his demeanor.

His gruff voice managed to block out the fear, to shove away the rising panic so that I could focus on him and his calming words.

I started to calm down.

I started to feel... safe.

But I don't feel safe now.

Nearly a half-dozen of the biggest people I've ever seen crowd into his living room, voices raised as angry, violent energy pours out of them. My terror returns full force, and I cower into the cushions, wishing I could sink right through them and disappear to the other side of the planet.

Ridge meets my eyes, a look of resignation passing through his amber irises. Then he pushes to his feet.

He's just as big as any of the men who've barged into the house, if not bigger. He wears a plain white t-shirt and Wranglers, but beneath those working man clothes, he has a body like I've never seen before: lean, muscular, broad shoulders and powerful legs. His ash-brown hair has a messy, unbrushed look that happens accidentally, and the close-cut beard gracing his jaw only heightens the scruffy wildness of his appearance.

He turns to face the newcomers, his boots shoulder-width apart and his hands dangling at his sides as he addresses the crowd. "Lawson. You ever heard of fuckin' knocking?"

Something about his pose tells me he's not casual—Ridge looks as if he could jerk into motion at any moment and put his fist through the big guy's face.

Lawson, the apparent leader of the group, puffs up his chest, his scowl deepening. "You brought an outsider into our village."

"What the fuck were you thinking?" another guy snaps. His question raises a rumble of agreement from the others.

"The pack wants answers." Lawson opens his palms

up as if to indicate the mob behind him. He's a little taller than Ridge, but he doesn't take up the room with just his presence like Ridge does. I have a feeling this guy is all show.

The thought doesn't really help me breathe past the looming panic attack though. He's still massive, with fists like ham hocks and an expression so full of loathing, I can't tell if he wants to get rid of me or Ridge. Possibly both.

"We're already facing a threat from the witches!" the only woman in the group snaps, raising her voice over the dull roar of the crowd. She's tall and formidable, muscles rippling in her golden brown arms. "And you drag this fucking carcass into our pack? You don't know that she isn't one of those wolf-hating assholes!"

I can't keep up with what they're saying. Panic has turned my heart into a fluttering bird in my chest, and their faces and voices are starting to blur together.

The pack? Witches? Wolf-hating?

None of this makes sense, and it's only exacerbating the fear I'd barely gotten past before they arrived. My panic is clawing its way back full force, stronger than it was before.

I try to hold it in, to control it and contain it. Ridge doesn't have any plans to hurt me—I'm sure of it. I saw something in his mesmerizing amber eyes before the mob arrived, a kind of protective warmth that barely made sense at the time. We don't know each other, but he wants to help me.

I believe him.

But voices are rising in anger. Six large people shouting at Ridge about putting the pack in danger, and Ridge facing them down with a stoic, expressionless face and low tones. He looks formidable, more dangerous than any of them could ever hope to be. But it's still six on one, and I don't want to be hurt anymore. I don't want anyone to be hurt.

I can't take more fucking violence. More anger.

My chest feels like it's being squeezed by a massive rubber band. I can't breathe.

As they continue screaming, I clutch at the couch cushions, trying not to fall into the panic attack I know is coming.

Everything that's happened to me in the last twenty-four hours is catching up to me—the fall down the stairs, seeing Doctor Patil, escaping my uncle, plunging into the ravine, waking up here in this strange cabin, and now this, these raised voices and the obvious animosity dangling in the air between my rescuer and Lawson.

What if Ridge *isn't* a nice guy? What if this is all a ruse by my uncle to hurt me? What if these people are going to tear me apart and scatter my pieces in the mountains?

My breaths come faster, ever more painful as I gasp for air. My gaze darts between the people yelling and back to

Ridge. I want him to make them go away. I want a chance to catch my breath, to figure out what the *hell* is going on.

Instead, I feel like I'm on the verge of a heart attack. My body is going to murder me before Clint or anyone else gets the chance.

Tensions soar higher, voices growing deeper and angrier, and suddenly, one of the men in the mob does something... strange. His body begins to morph, to change shape.

It only takes ten seconds, but in my current state of mind, it feels like it takes a lifetime. When it's over, where he stood on two legs before, a wolf stands in his place.

A large, growling wolf.

And I finally lose it.

The scream that comes from my lips is like nothing I've ever emitted in my entire life. Not even in the heat of Uncle Clint's punishments. Not even when I was little and hadn't taught myself to bear the pain, to go to another place inside my mind.

I scramble up onto the couch, still screaming, my legs tangling beneath me as I try to get my knees to work so I can run away. My heart pounds against my chest, frantic and demanding, trying to escape the terror inside me.

I see Ridge move. He reaches for me, but I can't hear his words. Then his face goes hard and he whips back around toward the waiting group, his hands clenching into fists at his side.

The wolf takes a few steps forward, snarling.

What the hell is happening? Why can't I wake up from this?

"Get the fuck out!" Ridge yells, his words the first sound to cut through my panic.

At his voice, I stop screaming, perched on the headrest of the couch, my fingernails digging into the corduroy. I gulp for breath, clinging to the sound of his deep baritone.

"Out!" Ridge snarls, shoving Lawson toward the door. The bigger man is thrown backward as if Ridge punched him, and he hits the wall hard, shaking the entire house. The wolf backs away with a yip as the other four people all cower a bit too. "And don't ever fucking question my authority again!"

The entire group scrambles away into the daylight, and Ridge leans out behind them, snarling, "Next time, fucking knock!" before he slams the door on their exit.

Then he looks back at me, and the fury on his face melts away as he strides across the room. He comes around the back of the couch, cupping my face in his hands. "Hey, shh. Shh, it's okay. They're gone. You're okay."

I'm still sucking in air like a drowning victim. I have tunnel-vision now, black edges sneaking in around my eyesight. Even his voice can't cut through this. I'm going to die of a heart attack, right here on the back of his couch like I'm a damn cat.

"Look at me." Ridge says gruffly, breaking through the

48

rush of noise in my head. I obey, clutching at his hands which still hold my face. "You're having a panic attack. What helps you through this?"

What helps?

A part of me recognizes that he knows this is normal for me. He knows I've done this before, again and again, my mind attempting to deal with the abuse that's become a normal part of my existence. And his perceptive gaze lays bare all of my secrets. It strikes me to my core. Someone knows the depth of my scars, and he wants to know what helps me deal with them.

My teeth chatter as I struggle to reply. "W-w-wat-ter."

He doesn't say anything else. Suddenly, I'm being lifted in his arms as if I'm just a child. I wrap my own arms around his neck, burying my face in his skin. There's that scent, the same woodsy pine scent I woke up to. I breathe it in, my tears soaking his t-shirt as he carries me through the house.

I keep my eyes closed and my face against the warmth of his skin, focusing on his scent because somehow it helps with the panic. So I only realize we're in the bathroom when I hear the snick of a shower curtain being opened. Then Ridge sets me down on my feet on a soft rug.

But I can't step away.

The thought of moving away from him sends another rush of panic through me, so I cling tighter. I don't even know quite why, but he's become my anchor in this storm, and I'm certain that if I lose my hold on him, I'll drown.

Ridge doesn't push me away. He doesn't mock me for my weakness or leave me to face the demons howling in my head on my own. Instead, he wraps an arm around my waist to hold me in place as he leans forward and turns on the water.

I know I'm going to have to let him go to get beneath the water. As he stands there testing the warmth of it with one hand, I brace myself for the impossible prospect of standing on my own.

But then his other arm comes around my waist, and I'm being lifted into the bathtub. Only... Ridge comes with me.

He managed to kick off his boots, I realize, without me even noticing. He sets me gently down on top of his bare feet, holding me tight to his body. We're both still fully clothed as the water cascades over us, and I don't loosen my grip on his neck.

Standing with him like this, I realize just how big he is compared to me. I'm leaning against him, my cheek resting against his broad chest. He drops his head so that his beard tickles my forehead, and his hands smooth gently over the back of my wet t-shirt, keeping me on my feet.

After a few moments, the panic begins to subside. Quicker than usual, even. Back home, in the aftermath of Clint's rage, I'd stand beneath the water for an hour, until all the warmth was gone and only cold remained, and still feel the effects of my panic attack.

But here, clinging to this stranger who smells like the mountains, this stranger who wants to help me, I find what might be the last scrap of peace inside myself.

My mind goes blank, and I just let the water fall around me, listening to the sound of his heartbeat beneath my ear.

7

SABLE

I WAKE FROM SLEEP GROGGILY, my eyelids blinking into clear, early morning light. The curtains on the window are drawn open, and I can see that Ridge closed the window back up sometime while I was asleep. His presence in the room while I slept sends a little shiver down my spine, despite the fact that he's done nothing but take care of me from the moment he brought me here.

Sleeping is such a vulnerable time.

And I'm terrified of being vulnerable with anyone.

I shove back the covers and gently sit up. My body is stiff and unwieldy, my limbs as heavy as my eyelids, and I scoot back to rest against the headboard and get my bearings. I don't remember getting out of the shower or falling asleep, but that's not abnormal for my panic attacks. When my mind goes blank at the tail end of an attack, I operate on autopilot.

I'm wearing some of Ridge's clothes again. A soft, worn pair of cotton shorts and a t-shirt three times too big for me. I realize I'm not wearing a bra or underwear, and I hope to God I took them off myself in the moments after my fully-clothed shower. I hope I changed my own clothes last night, because Ridge already did it once—and that time, he at least kept my underwear on. If I didn't change myself last night, then he certainly got an eyeful of my body.

The thought sends a new wave of panic skittering through me, but on the heels of that, there's something else. Something warm. A tingle that travels through my belly, making my breath hitch a little. I can't quite identify the feeling, but it floods my cheeks with heat.

Regardless of who changed me after the shower, I feel weirdly safe here in Ridge's bed, wearing his clothes. But I don't want to hold on to the feeling.

As far as I'm concerned, nowhere is safe. Not here, not the hospital, not back home with my uncle. Life with Clint taught me that people are fundamentally bad and want to hurt me. It's just human nature to want to hurt each other.

If I expect anything else, I put myself right back in danger.

The cobwebs of sleep continue to slowly recede from my mind, and as they do, I realize something else is different. I'm no longer wearing my wrist brace.

My arm, which ached like a son of a bitch yesterday, barely hurts. My ankle feels better too. Some of the bruises and scrapes I gathered during my flight through the woods are barely visible anymore, although the scars my uncle left on me are still there.

I blink, my throat tightening convulsively.

How long was I asleep for?

There's a brief knock at the door, then Ridge calls through the thick wood, "Are you awake? I brought breakfast."

My heart skips a beat, and for a moment, I think I'm about to have yet another damn panic attack. But then I realize that's not it at all. It's his voice making my heart skip, and in a way I'm not accustomed to.

"I'm awake," I call out, my voice scratchy and rough.

"May I come in?"

I'm floored by the question. Uncle Clint would have just barged in—*it's my fucking house, kid.* Ridge is giving me the option to turn him away, something I was never allowed back home.

All I can manage is a strangled, "Yes!" that comes out a little too high-pitched as a strange mix of emotions flood my chest.

The door opens, and Ridge walks in holding a small tray that bears a steaming mug and a plate. His ash-brown hair is rumpled and the black t-shirt he's wearing molds to his muscles, giving him a strong, dangerous air that makes my heart rate ratchet. I have to remind myself he's a friend who has no intention of hurting me.

Even so, when he gives me a tentative smile, his honeyed eyes on mine as he sets the tray over my legs, panic rears its ugly head.

"I hope you like eggs and bacon," he says, taking a seat on the edge of the bed. "It's all I had."

His closeness strikes a chord of leftover terror in me. Coupled with the panic, it sends me into a spiral, and I scoot away, sloshing coffee over the edge of the mug as I jar the tray with my legs.

Ridge's eyes soften, and he gets up, walking to the pile of laundry in the corner where he extracts a dirty shirt. He keeps his movements slow and both of his hands in my field of vision as he mops up the spilled coffee.

"I didn't know if you liked milk and sugar in your coffee," he says, carefully dabbing up the last of the liquid. "So I brought you both."

I swallow hard as he moves away. He tosses the shirt back into the laundry pile, then moves to the very bottom of the bed, choosing the side that puts him as far away from me as possible.

A lump rises in my throat at his generosity, and at the way he seems to understand what I need just from my crazy reactions. The rapid thudding of my heart slows, and as it does, my stomach lets out an unholy growl.

Jesus. How long has it actually been since I last ate? I've lost track of time almost completely, but this is the second day I've woken up in this man's bed. He must've gotten me to at least drink some water after my panic attack yesterday, because my mouth doesn't feel too dry and cottony.

Ridge gives me a gentle, somewhat amused smile as I press a hand over my stomach. The way one corner of his lips tilts a little higher than the other makes him look rugged and slightly rough around the edges, just like everything else about him.

Dragging my gaze away from his full lips, I reach out and tentatively pick up a piece of bacon. The plate is a plain turquoise with a darker bottom and looks handmade, while the small coffee mug declares MONTANA in bold lettering, with an artistic rendering of the state's natural features below that. Neither dish goes together aesthetically, yet somehow, they work.

"What's your name?" Ridge asks softly, drawing my attention back to him.

I hesitate, then bite into the bacon, tearing off half the strip. I take my time chewing, my gaze fixed on the steam rising from my mug. I'm not sure I should tell him my name, although I can't exactly pinpoint where that worry comes from.

What kind of power would he have over me if I did? What if Clint has missing person posters up and Ridge turns me over?

But some tiny part of me that goes against my own sense of self-preservation wants to trust this man.

Something inside me is drawn to him, feels safe with him—almost as if I've known him for years instead of less than forty-eight hours.

I swallow my bacon past a throat that's gone dry as the desert, then flick my gaze up to meet his as I say, "I'm Sable."

Ridge's eyes darken as he hears my name, the amber color shifting to a hue like burnished gold, and the change sends another tingle over me. Exactly how I felt when I thought of him seeing me naked when he changed my clothes. Something warm and intoxicating deep in my body.

I know what it is, I think. It's just not something I've ever really felt before.

And I still have no idea what it means. So I deflect with the most burning question I've had since yesterday afternoon.

"Was it real?" I ask, reaching for another strip of bacon. "The wolf in your living room? He was a man... and then he was a wolf."

Ridge narrows his eyes at me, not in anger like Uncle Clint used to, but as if he's carefully constructing his next statement. I can't really blame him for seeming to walk on eggshells around me—I haven't proven to be the most stable of individuals since he opened his home to me. Even now, balancing on this precarious ledge where he's about to tell me whether I hallucinated that or not, I'm on the borderline of losing my nerve again.

"What you saw really happened," he finally says, clearly deciding not to try to sugarcoat or dance around the truth.

I suck in a breath, putting the bacon back down quickly before my shaking fingers drop it on the clean sheets. "Jesus."

"I need you to understand that you're safe here," he rushes to add. He places a palm on the mattress between us, as if he wishes he could place it on my arm in comfort. I manage to keep myself from shrinking away again, although maybe that's just because my brain is too busy trying to wrap its head around what he just told me.

"Are you... a wolf too?"

The words come out strangled. The first revelation already threatened to overwhelm me, but if the answer to this is yes...

I have an itch to run. Again. How can I be safer in the hands of weird man-wolf hybrids than I would be alone in the wilderness?

"Yes, I'm a wolf shifter. But we're not a threat to you." Ridge's deep voice is calm and measured. "We pose no threat to human communities. My pack is peaceful. We keep to ourselves mostly, and we keep our existence secret from ordinary humans. It's safer for everybody that way."

Threatened with an overload of emotion, I focus on the

one thing that really sticks out. *"Your* pack. There's more than one pack?"

"There used to be four. But we're down to three after —" He breaks off, shaking his head. "There are only three now."

I don't know what he was about to say, but questions are crowding my mind, clogging my brain as they pile up on top of each other. It's hard for me to keep hold of a single train of thought for too long as I try to process everything that's happened to me.

Holding up my left hand, I wiggle the fingers, surprised all over again that I can do it without pain. "What happened to my wrist? It was... it was hurt. Sprained. And my ankle..."

"Yeah." Ridge's eyes harden, but I don't think the anger in them is directed at me. "I had our healer come take a look at your injuries. She was able to patch up the worst of them, including your arm and your ankle." His brows pull together, and he scans my body quickly. "Are you hurt anywhere else? I can bring her back if you are."

"No. No, I'm okay."

I really don't feel pain anywhere else, and I'm relieved to hear that the healer is a woman. But I don't think I could handle being touched or examined by another stranger right now.

"All right." Ridge leans back a little, a look of relief crossing his face. "Well, just tell me if—"

He cuts off, turning away from me and craning his ear toward the window. The glass is closed, and I don't hear anything for several seconds.

Then a chorus of howls pierce the silence, faint in the distance but loud enough for me to pick up on.

"Fuck me," Ridge growls, standing abruptly. He shoves a hand through his messy brown hair, then drags his palm down his face, closing his eyes as if to brace himself. When he opens his eyes, he levels that honey gaze on me, grimacing slightly. "I have to go."

I nod, though I feel a twinge of regret that he's leaving when we've only just begun talking. If I learn more about his pack, and about the life they lead, I think maybe I won't feel the need to run so fast and far.

Life with Clint was one long unknown. Would I get a day's respite before he raised a hand to me again? Would he feed me? Would he let me read a book so that I could have an escape from the horror that was my life?

The answers to those questions varied daily, and it kept me in a permanent state of high alert, my nervous system braced for whatever might come.

Here in Ridge's secluded cabin, I'm still facing an unknown, and maybe that's why I can't calm down. I'm tired of the unknown. I want a plan, I want *certainty*, and I want to feel like I'm in control of my life.

He's already crossing the room and opening the door,

moving quickly. But he stops with his hand on the doorknob and turns back, his dark brow furrowed.

"You're not a prisoner, Sable," he says. "You aren't my captive in any way, and I have no intention of keeping you here against your will."

"O-okay."

I nod my head a few shakes too many before I finally get it to stop, and a flush creeps up my cheeks.

Way to go, Sable. Just keep proving how insane you are to the beautiful man who's doing his best to help you.

Ridge opens the door more and takes another step, but he's still looking at me as he adds, "But if you stay here, you'll be safe. I promise."

Then he disappears through the door, leaving it open behind him.

8

RIDGE

It takes a lot of fucking willpower to leave that door open.

What I really want to do is slam it shut and barricade it closed so that the woman in my bedroom can't leave. Just because I told her she was free to go doesn't mean I want her to. I want to keep her right here with me, where I know some jackass isn't putting out cigarettes on her perfect skin.

What the fuck is wrong with me?

The front door slams shut behind me as I step out of the cabin, and I shove my hands in my pockets as I stride down the front walk to the packed-dirt road. I don't know why I want so fucking much for Sable to stay with me. She's nobody to me. Some chick I found half-dead in a ravine, and to hear my brother bitch about it, I should have left her there.

But as I walk away from my cabin, the thought that she

might actually leave while I'm gone makes me sick to my stomach.

For now, though, this council meeting is a lot more pressing than keeping Sable in my bed. If Lawson caught a whiff of me putting a woman before my duties to the pack, he'd use it as a reason to wrest the pack out from under my control.

Not that he'd need a lot of reason to want to try.

Since I won out over him in the fight for alpha status, he's been waiting for his chance to prove he's smarter, stronger, and better. To prove that my winning was some kind of fluke.

The escalation of witch violence in recent weeks has left all three packs in a constant state of vigilance and worry. Just last week, the East Pack lost three wolves in a coordinated attack that decimated a couple acres of their territory and left them nothing to bury but pieces. It's more imperative than ever that we band together to defeat the witch threat, which means I've got to get my head in the game and forget about Sable. For the next hour, at least.

Beyond that? I'm not sure it'll be possible.

I hear a crunch of feet behind me before Grady O'Connell steps into view beside me, falling into step with my long strides. Grady reminds me of Mr. Clean, with a bald head that reflects the sunlight and deeply tanned skin. He's as big as the cleaning mascot, too, six-foot-four at least with muscles that are at odds with his beer habit. He has one hand up to shield his eyes from the sun, and the other wrapped around a Coors Light that's condensing in the late morning warmth.

"Ridge." He grins at me, a knowing smirk that lets me know he probably saw the entire fucking debacle with Sable earlier. "You wanna talk about it?"

"Fuck off," I growl, but I smile anyway. Grady's a nice guy—two decades older than me and once a good friend of my father's. He's a little on the eccentric side, but he's a good man who's never once questioned my authority since I won alpha status after my father's death five years ago.

"Never figured you for the kinda man who'd have to drag a woman home. She's cute though," Grady goes on, clucking his teeth as if to punctuate his statement. "Nice ass."

I shoot a glare in his direction, my head turning toward him sharply. I know he's kidding. He's a happily mated man, and he's more interested in giving me shit than in checking out a girl's ass.

Still, it doesn't change the warning in my tone. "Keep your paws off her."

He laughs. "Oh, I plan to. You know we've got some eligible bachelorettes of our own though, right? You don't have to go pickin' up strange women and bringin' them back—"

I pause and kick a cloud of dirt in his direction, earning a laugh in return. "Thought I told you to fuck off?"

"All right, all right," he says, holding up both hands in surrender. Then his smile fades. "But in all seriousness, I wanted to let you know I found evidence of campfires out on the Rim this morning during patrol."

"Shit." I stop, gravel shifting beneath my boots as I turn to face him. "New?"

"Fresh," Grady says grimly. "Still smoking."

"They're getting braver."

"Or stupider," he points out.

"Either way, that's the closest they've come on our lands in a while." I stare off at the trees, at the sun riding high over the mountains. What would my father have done if he'd lived long enough to see the witches grow this bold in their war on us? "What are our options here?" I say under my breath, avoiding Grady's concerned gaze. "We're fighting an entire race of supernatural beings that wants to eradicate us because we're 'aberrations' of magic."

"In their opinion," the older man grumbles.

"In their opinion alone," I agree. "So what do we do? Wipe them out before they can wipe us out? Try to bridge the gap? Prove to them that the fact we use magic to shift doesn't make us anything less than them?"

Grady knocks back a swig of his Coors before he says, "You can't use logic with people who're talking genocide. The only thing you can do is fight fire with fire."

"Magic with magic." I sigh and look back at the old man. "Nice talk. Now fuck off."

"You've always been so eloquent. You didn't get that from your dad," Grady chuckles. Then he gives me a clap on the shoulder and heads off toward home.

The council meets in the largest building in town—a long, low, corrugated metal barn that's blisteringly hot in summer and icy in winter.

Several members of the East Pack are milling around outside the barn with a few of my own wolves, and they all greet me with brief nods before continuing their conversations. Each of the packs send their alpha plus a handful of council members to each meeting, and they're typically familiar faces—like Archer, the quiet golden boy of the East Pack who's been standing in for his ailing father, the alpha. Our gazes meet, and I acknowledge him with a polite nod but keep walking.

I'm barely through the door into the dim interior before Amora appears from the shadows and latches on to my arm, dragging me right back outside. You wouldn't know it by looking at her long, lean figure, but the woman's got a grip like a fucking vise.

The sunlight reflects off a hard glint in her vivid green eyes as she releases me and hisses quietly, "All right, what the fuck is going on? Lawson damn near busted down your door, and now he's telling anybody who'll listen that you have a witch holed up in your house."

Amora's been my closest friend and confidante since we were kids, and even more so since I took over the pack.

She balances the rage inside of me, dishing out her no-nonsense logic when I need it most.

I shake my arm free of her clutches and snort. "A witch? Really?"

Her long, dark ponytail swishes as she shrugs. "That's what he's saying. Most of us don't believe him, but you know he has his fanboys."

"She's not a witch." A growl rumbles in my chest, my gaze darting around the lawn as if Lawson might be standing close enough for me to shove my fist through his face. "We'd smell it."

"Would we?" Amora asks simply. "We don't really have a precedent for that, do we? If we could scent the magic in them, it would make defending against them a hell of a lot easier."

"She's *not*," I insist.

Amora crosses her arms and peers down her nose at me in a look so reminiscent of our childhood it almost makes me laugh. "How about you just tell me where she came from, and we'll go from there?"

"I found her at the bottom of Devil's Ditch. Unconscious."

Her eyebrows shoot up. "What's her story?"

"I don't know!" I snap, throwing my hands in the air. "I can't get a fucking moment alone with her to ask!"

Some of the East Pack members are staring at me, their attention drawn by my outburst. Amora glances at them, then latches on to my elbow and drags me around the edge of the barn, out of sight. She lets me go with a little shove of irritation. "Would you chill? You're acting like a crazy person."

I open my mouth, ready to go on the defensive, then snap my jaws shut with an audible click of my teeth and rub away the bruising she's left on my arm. Amora's right. And to be honest, I feel like a fucking crazy person too. Ever since I dragged Sable home with me. I don't know what's going on with me. Maybe I'm hiding it well from everyone else—even from myself—but I've never been able to hide anything from Amora.

"Ridge, listen to me." My friend steeples her fingers in front of her face as if she's praying and waits until I've given her my undivided attention. "You're violating the packs' treaty by allowing an unsanctioned being to reside in your house."

I clench my jaw at the unwelcome reminder and nod once. I'm lucky Grady's an easygoing old fart, or he would've been on my ass for letting in an outsider instead of just giving me shit about my skills with women.

"Our treaty declares that all three packs have agreed to close ourselves off from newcomers," Amora goes on.

"Like I don't fucking know?" I grunt.

"Well, clearly, you don't." Amora arches a brow, pointing in the direction of my cabin. "Because there's an unsanctioned female on your couch."

I almost correct her with, *In my bed, actually,* but that seems like it would open a whole new can of fucking worms. I've had enough drama in the last twenty-four hours to last me for the rest of my damn life.

"Trust is in short supply lately," Amora says, oblivious to my inner thoughts. Thank God. "Half the pack already thinks you've gone off the deep end and put us in danger. What happens when the other packs find out? You think Trystan is gonna stand for this? Or even Archer?"

I know she's right, but the reminder is frustrating as fuck. Treaty be damned. I can't just kick Sable out of my house. Not in the state she's in. But even more than that—I have no fucking clue why, but I can't let her go.

"I just... need a minute," I growl in a low voice. "A day, some time to figure out why she was abandoned, beat to shit, in the middle of our territory."

"Maybe because she's a plant?" Amora suggests. "Put there by the witches to infiltrate our pack?"

My jaw clenches, and so do my fists.

"She's not. We don't have time to stand here and argue. We have a meeting."

I stalk away before Amora can say anything else. I hate how often our conversations end in me walking away because I don't like what her logic has to say. She's never sugarcoated her opinions for me or been anything but blunt and honest—and the truth is, I'm a better man because of the times I listened to her.

But this…

What if she's right?

Yes, Sable has clearly been the victim of abuse. Nobody can fake all those scars that look as if they span at least a decade's worth of time. But that doesn't mean she wasn't chosen explicitly by the witches to infiltrate our pack. My gut knows it's not true—I can look in the girl's haunted gray-blue eyes and know there's no malice there, and there's definitely no magic.

Regardless, Amora has planted a worry I wish I didn't have to carry.

Then again, maybe it won't even have a chance to be an issue. I told the golden-haired angel she wasn't my prisoner. That she was free to leave if she chose.

As I walk into the dark interior of the council building, I rub the ache in my chest and wonder if Sable's already gone.

9

SABLE

THE CABIN IS calm and silent after Ridge leaves. I finish the bacon before moving on to the scrambled eggs, and even though the meal is as simple as it can get, it's delicious —the bacon just the right amount of crispy, the eggs fluffy and moist. It hits the spot for me in a way no food has in a very long time.

From what I've been able to tell, Ridge definitely lives alone in this small cabin. I'm touched that he went out of his way to cook me breakfast and to bring it to me in bed. He also wasn't half bad at trying to be as non-threatening as possible. And I appreciate that too.

That doesn't mean you should stay, I think as I finish off my cooling coffee and put the empty mug back on the tray.

But I'm torn. On the one hand, my fight-or-flight

impulse has taken up what feels like permanent residence in my gut, and every nerve-ending in my body is screaming at me to run. Ignoring that self-preservation instinct that's become so ingrained in me after life with my uncle feels like the stupidest thing I could possibly do right now.

But on the other hand... I'd be safe here. Safer than anywhere else. I truly believe that now, at least.

After I finish, I carry the tray into the kitchen and spend a few minutes washing and drying the dishes, before I open every cabinet and drawer in the room to put them away in the right place. I figure if Ridge is going to cook for me, the proper thing for me to do is at least clean up after myself.

His kitchen is small, tucked in a corner adjacent to the living room with one small window over the metal sink and a back door that opens out over a small empty plot of grass. The cabinets are mostly empty—just a handful of plates, bowls, cups, and mugs, which tells me he doesn't have company over often. The fridge is sparse too. A gallon of milk, eggs, bacon, and lunch meat with a few generic condiments. Because I'm nosy, I also open the freezer and find it packed full with different kinds of meat, which I guess shouldn't be surprising given he's a wolf.

A wolf.

Holy fuck, I still can't quite believe that.

Closing the freezer, I walk through the living room and

poke around a bit. There are three magazines on the solid wooden coffee table—two copies of *Men's Health* and a single copy of *Popular Mechanics* that advertises "How to Survive the Next Great Disaster."

Funny. I could use some advice in that regard in my own life.

Other than the couch and coffee table, the living room area is sparse, but with a clean, masculine feel. The hardwood floors look freshly varnished and shine beneath the rays of sunlight slanting through the double picture window. I pass back into the hallway where a coat rack holds several jackets.

I hesitate for a second before pressing my face into a blue jean jacket lined with flannel and taking a deep breath of Ridge's unique woodsy scent.

Then a flush creeps up my neck, and I glance guiltily toward the door as if expecting him to come bursting through demanding to know why I'm sniffing his clothes like some kind of creepy stalker.

I wouldn't have an answer for him. Not one that makes sense anyway. I just know that I can't get enough of the way he smells. The way his voice sounds. The way his amber eyes burn like two steady, reassuring flames.

Even just the lingering scent of his jacket in my nostrils brings me a kind of calm I never knew existed.

I take one more surreptitious sniff, promising myself

this is the last one, before continuing on in my exploration of the house.

A woven throw rug in shades of brown and tan rests by the front door, and I pause, the soft weave plush beneath my bare toes as I tiptoe to peek out the high decorative window in the door.

At first glance, the street outside looks empty. The bedroom is on the opposite side of the house, and I ran down a small dirt road lined by other houses when I ran for the woods yesterday. On this side, a larger gravel road runs just beyond the small front yard, and other similar cabins sit on the other side of the street.

I'm tempted to slip on shoes and step outside to get a better look at this little settlement. It looks like a miniature version of Big Creek, which is a small town in its own right, and I wonder how it functions so far from civilization.

But before I can make a move, I notice a group of big, burly men striding through the village.

I duck, my heart rate jumping. I saw no indication they were coming here—the five or six men looked as if they were deep in conversation, faces and movements relaxed as they navigated up the road. But something about them pokes the fear that's lain right beneath the surface in me since the moment I awoke in Ridge's house, never entirely fading away no matter what I do.

Those men passing by the cabin are huge, powerful,

dominant. Just like the ones who burst into the house yesterday.

Just like all of these people.

These wolves.

These *shifters*.

I don't quite understand what it means for someone to be a shifter, besides the fact that they can change from human to animal and back. I don't know what it all means.

But I recognize strength, power, and dominance when I see it.

And all I can think of is Uncle Clint.

For so long, I was kept captive in his house. I had no identity or autonomy. Even as fearful as I've been during my time here, I've never felt as scared as I was living under Clint's roof. I've tasted the possibility of freedom and the possibility of finally being my own person, and I absolutely refuse to give that up. I refuse to be my uncle's captive any longer.

But I refuse to be a captive here either.

I can't stay.

I jam my feet into my shoes—which Ridge has left by the door—and then race toward the kitchen, my laces trailing on the ground. I slam through the back door and out into the tiny backyard, veering away from the garden shed and toward the dark line of forest beyond the dead end road. The same escape route I tried and failed to take last time.

The men out front are speaking in loud voices, and I cringe as I halt by the edge of the road and look around for anybody who might see me sneaking away.

A small part of me knows this is asinine. Ridge doesn't want to hurt me. He promised he'd keep me safe, and his cabin is definitely preferable to a cave in the wild.

But I think of that group of furious people barreling into his living room and the new men I saw striding past his cabin. I think of the way that wolf's teeth glinted as it growled. I think of how fucking out of my depth I am in all of this, how outnumbered and vulnerable I am here, and my fear ramps into unnatural, uncontrollable, completely illogical territory.

I see nobody, so I fall into a sprint, one hand wrapped around the waistband of Ridge's shorts to keep them from falling off as I hurry toward the forest. Too late now to go back and find my own clothes, which are likely clean in Ridge's laundry room because he's just so damn kind.

I don't have time for going back. I have to move forward. I have to be free.

The woods beckon like a shadow beacon of hope. I'm nearing the edge of the road, about to leap off the flat dirt and into the grass, when a hand like iron wraps around my bicep and yanks me back.

I let out a squeaky yelp as my body comes to a vicious halt before I'm jerked back onto the road. Everything whirls around me as I'm yanked around, and then suddenly, the man called Lawson is looming over me, his fingers cutting off circulation in my arm.

Terror makes my legs weak, and I collapse to the dirt on my knees, dangling from his grip.

He glares at me, looking every bit as intimidating as when he challenged Ridge yesterday.

"I knew you couldn't be trusted, you fucking liar," he spits, giving me a shake that rattles the fillings in my teeth. "You spying on us? About to run back to your little coven and tell them our secrets?"

"P-please. Please let me go." My words come out small and shaky, wobbly from the force of his shaking, and I try to pull away from his rock-hard grip.

His eyes narrow. This man is the complete opposite of Ridge, with dusky blond hair and blue eyes. He has a face that would be attractive if it weren't filled with so much vicious anger, and he's the size of a small house. I swear he's channeling the strength of ten men in his grasp on my arm.

"No, I don't think I will." He scowls. "I think the council needs to meet you. I think you need to be made an example of to all your bitch, wolf-hating friends."

"Please." My voice is hardly more than a breath, and I feel a rush of shame at how terrified and tearful I sound. "I don't want any trouble. I'm leaving. I just want to go."

He sneers. "Yeah? Tell that to your executioners."

Without another word, Lawson literally drags me

through the village by my arm as my legs scrape uselessly against the ground. Thank God the roads aren't concrete, and only dust and gravel grates on my bare skin, but the pain is still unbearable given all my other injuries, and he's moving too fast for me to get my feet beneath me. At least he's not hauling me by my sprained wrist, or the agony would be even more excruciating.

By the time we reach a metal barn on the outskirts of the village, I'm sobbing. His grip has made my arm numb, and I'm almost certain he's wrenched it hard enough to pull muscles and ligaments. I'm wishing I never left Ridge's house, that I'd been smart enough to stay put and keep out of sight.

If Lawson has his way, I'll be lynched on sight.

He slams open the door to the barn with more force than necessary, and I yank against his hold in a last-ditch, desperate effort to get away. His other hand sinks into my hair and he grabs a handful, dragging me by the roots into a large open space rimmed by astonished faces.

We reach the central area, and Lawson throws me onto the concrete floor. I slam into the ground, barely keeping my head from making contact with the concrete, and cry out as my sprained wrist takes too much of the blow.

The room is silent. Dozens of faces stare at me, just as surprised at my arrival as I am.

Shifters, I realize with another wave of terror. *I'm surrounded by shifters.*

Nobody moves, nobody even seems to breathe, and all I can hear is the rushing in my ears and the unnatural pounding in my chest.

Today is the day I die. After everything Uncle Clint did to me, I never thought it would end like this.

10

TRYSTAN

THESE COUNCIL MEETINGS are a waste of my goddamned time.

But I come to them because that's what I'm supposed to do. The alpha plays nice with the other packs. The alpha builds bridges and shakes hands and kisses rancid ass to ensure cooperation between them and us. Inter-pack cooperation and all that stupid bullshit.

That doesn't mean I have to like it.

I hate this drafty barn the North Pack has built out of recycled materials and spit, and I especially hate listening to fucking Ridge Harcourt droning on about trespassers on their land, or Archer from the East Pack talking about his sick father.

Their problems are real, and they have my sympathies —but their problems aren't *my* problems. My pack is doing fine. We're handling the witch threat, beefing up our own security, and not for the first time, I'm spending every boring second of this meeting wondering what the fuck I'm doing here.

The West Pack has never been stronger. My pack hasn't lost a wolf yet, and those goddamned witches haven't trampled the slightest blade of grass on our lands. These two are the ones who can't protect their packs. I'd rather be back home taking care of my people than standing here watching Ridge's expressionless face drone on about recently lit campfires near the boundary.

So I'm catatonic as if I've been drugged, holding up the wall as if it's my mission in life and trying desperately not to fall asleep.

One of my advisors elbows me every time I nod off, and irritation burns in my chest every time he does, but he's got a point. I need to play nice unless I want to make enemies of the other packs. I may be a cocky asshole—hell, I'd be the first to admit that's exactly what I am—but I take the protection of my people seriously. And maintaining good relations is part of that, as boring as it may be.

But my boredom is quickly shoved away when the door bursts open, slamming into the wall so hard the whole rickety shack quivers.

Lawson appears in the doorway, all bulk and no brains with a shadowy figure dangling from his hand.

The edges of my lips curl up, and I fight the inherent urge to snarl at the North Pack alpha's younger brother.

Lawson is as cocky as I am, but he's got no fucking class, the kind of giant tornado that can do damage to a city but can't wipe his own ass.

Even my people know he's been trying to steal the pack out from under Ridge since their father died. I'm not a big fan of Ridge with his serious, holier-than-thou attitude, but I *really* don't like Lawson. He's a sociopath in wolf's skin, and that ticking time bomb is set to blow at the worst possible time.

The blond man storms into the barn and throws the second figure onto the floor. He crosses his arms over his broad chest before turning to address his brother with a smirk.

"Found your whore trying to sneak away," Lawson says, his deep voice booming through the room like a gunshot. "Did it ever occur to you when you brought her onto pack land that she might run away to her friends and tell them all our secrets? Since you're here and I found her trying to run off into the woods a few minutes ago, I assume that means you left this *witch* alone in your damn house."

The entire council react to that bomb, people surging to their feet as a ripple goes through the gathered crowd. Loud voices rise around me, every face turning to Ridge for answers.

But I exchange glances with Archer, the East Pack's acting alpha. I may not like Lawson, but I doubt the ass-hat would walk into a council meeting and accuse his alpha—and his brother—of bringing an unsanctioned visitor onto pack lands if he didn't have proof to back it up. Not to mention the inflammatory implication she's a witch.

If all this is true, that means Ridge broke the treaty, and now Archer and myself have to clean up the mess.

Fuck, as if having to come to these meetings isn't bullshit enough, now I have to do damage control?

The grumblings get louder, nearly all of it directed at Ridge, who's staring stone-faced at his brother. Instead of joining the growing number of dissenters, I level my gaze on the girl.

She's small and petite, probably a few years younger than I am—all wide eyes and delicate limbs with so much fear rolling off her, you'd think Lawson had jammed a knife against her throat. Not that he's been anything but a raging asshole since he dragged her in here, but her level of fear makes it seem like she thinks she's about to die.

The woman looks like she wants to curl into a ball small enough to disappear into the floor. My jaw clenches as Lawson grabs her once more and yanks her to her feet, yelling at his brother about breaking the treaty.

The woman doesn't just let him manhandle her again though. She gets her feet underneath her and yanks away from Lawson's iron grip with a low, breathy shout.

"Let go of me, asshole!"

My eyebrows twitch upward in surprise, and even Lawson looks a little shocked.

Huh. Little thing's got a backbone under all that fear.

Her wide blue eyes are feral, her gaze darting around as if she's cataloguing every person in the room while also seeking out the nearest exit. I watch her clock the door Lawson left wide open behind them, and how the crowd of council members isn't blocking her route of escape. She searches the crowd on either side, and I can almost taste the way she's weighing her odds of getting past us. Can she outrun us? Can she reach the forest and disappear?

Sorry, hot stuff. There's not a chance in hell you can outrun and outsmart wolves.

I think she knows it too. But before she comes to any kind of decision on whether to try anyway, her gaze meets mine.

The weight of that gaze hits me like a falling boulder off a ravine.

Something pulls hard and almost painfully inside me, and my wolf growls. Beneath the protective snarl, I feel something so raw and visceral that I can't even believe it's happening.

Mine.

I shove away from the wall, my eyes widening as my wolf howls inside me.

She's mine.

"You know the rules. You signed the treaty yourself.

She doesn't belong here, Ridge," one of the North Pack's advisors is saying, trying to maintain some semblance of orderly discourse. "She can't stay here, regardless of what state you found her in."

"She's not a witch," Ridge growls. "She needs help. Are we to just turn our backs on anybody who stumbles onto our land beaten and bloody?"

"We are when there's an entire race of beings trying to destroy us."

"The witch needs to be locked up," another voice chimes in. "We need to make sure we're safe from her. Then we'll discuss what to do with her."

The blonde woman's gaze is still locked on mine, her expression a little dazed. Then she shakes her head as if to clear it, dragging her focus away from me. She darts a wild-eyed glance at the door again as the council argues with Ridge.

How has no one felt that ocean of terror rolling off her? How can they not see how frightened and vulnerable she is?

The wolf inside me is raging to get to her, to wrap his body around her and protect her from these assholes.

Before I even realize what I'm doing, I take two strides forward. This isn't normal—Trystan, alpha of the West Pack, having fuck-all to say during a council meeting. I certainly don't put myself on display like this, and that's evident in the way people abruptly stop talking and look at me like I've grown a second head.

"That woman is a wolf," I say, pitching my voice loud enough to be heard over the low grumble of unease still filling the room. "I know it as sure as I know my own name."

Ridge cocks his head at me, though his face doesn't change. I can see the thoughts working in his head—he's trying to figure out my endgame, what I get out of saying such a thing and fighting for this strange woman.

Before I can speak again and declare her my mate, Archer comes forward, joining me in the center of the room.

"It's true," he says, and his quiet voice is stronger than I've ever heard it. He's a pretty boy with gold hair and green eyes, and if his father wasn't back home dying, he wouldn't even be here. But he motions to the woman and says again, "Trystan's right. I know she's a wolf, because my wolf has claimed her as its mate."

Shock thrums through me, making the back of my neck prickle as hackles try to rise even in my human form. What the fuck? How is that possible?

My wolf has claimed her.

She's mine.

But Archer clearly doesn't think so.

Across the room, Ridge lets out a long, low growl that leaves no room for interpretation.

11

SABLE

RIDGE'S GROWL FINALLY FADES, but I swear I can hear an echo of it bouncing off the stark walls of the large building.

The room has grown so silent, I feel as if I can hear every breath being taken. Beyond the breathing, I can also feel the weight of every gaze latched on to me, made heavier by the thick tension that clogs the air.

I don't like being the center of attention like this. I don't like all these eyes on me—not Ridge's concerned gaze or Lawson's pissed off one or any of the different levels of emotion in between.

My heart pounds with such force that I'm sure every predator here can hear it or sense the blood pumping overtime through my veins. I stand with my feet shoulder width apart, ready to run at the first glimpse of violence, even as fear threatens to turn my knees to jelly. Lawson left the door open, and I will absolutely make my escape if it looks like my only option.

Two nights ago, I decided to live life on my terms for once.

If it comes to it, I'll die on my terms too.

The beautiful blond man with the soft voice stands closer to me than most, and his expression is calm even as he stares down the rest of the crowd. He looks gentle and not at all like the hard, angry shifters around us.

But of all the people in the barn, he's the one I'm most afraid of right now.

My wolf has claimed her as its mate.

What does that mean?

What kind of crazy cult have I walked into?

"You're wrong." Ridge's voice is like gunfire in the silence. He steps forward, irritation flashing across his face. He looks even more intense than he did in the moment when he kicked the mob out of his living room. "She cannot be your mate. My wolf has already claimed her."

My heart lurches in my chest, and if it weren't for the fact that my feet are rooted to the floor, I might fall over.

Ridge's amber gaze seeks mine, and I can sense him trying to calm me. He must know I'm about three breaths away from another panic attack.

Despite everything, despite my fear and confusion and rising hysteria, my body responds to him like it has every other time. I drink in that soothing look, my mind going back to last night and the scent of his skin, his wet shirt beneath my cheek, his heartbeat steady in my ear.

Buoyed by the reminder, I set a firmer stance and shove away the fear that tightens my throat.

The first man who spoke inches farther into the open circle in the middle of the barn-like structure. He has chocolate brown hair and vivid blue eyes tinted green like the ocean. I recognize him by sight—he was one of the big shifters walking down the street that frightened me so much I ran. He carries himself with a kind of lazy, predatory lean that says he's highly comfortable in his own skin.

Turning those blue-green eyes on Ridge, he shakes his head. "That's not possible. My wolf has claimed her."

"Then it's equally not possible for your wolf to do so when mine already has." Ridge glances around the room as if to check that everyone's attention is on him before he says, "I found this woman two nights ago, half-dead in Devil's Ditch. I was compelled to help her, though I didn't understand at first why." His expression softens as he turns to look at me, something I can't even name burning behind his amber irises. "But it makes sense. My wolf knew before I did that she belongs to me."

His words are like a match to dry tinder, setting off a flurry of emotions inside my chest.

Panic.

Confusion.

Anger.

And a strange sort of thrill.

I don't understand what the hell is going on here, and I have to fight down the urge to scream my frustration to the heavens. To lash out recklessly like an animal trapped in a net.

I'm not so stupid as to be unaware of how tenuous my position is right now. Any one of these creatures could rip me limb from limb, and the unfortunate truth is several of them look ready to do just that. I don't know what the hell is going on with Ridge and these two strange men all arguing that they have some kind of claim on me, but at the moment, it's the only thing keeping teeth away from my skin.

So despite the fact that I'm still terrified and confused, I stay silent and wait it out.

The rest of the group isn't so startled into silence, however, and a steady rumble of low voices starts up amidst the crowd.

Ridge and the other two men attempting to "claim" me face off against one another. Their faces grow thunderous as they stare one another down, and I know without a doubt they're ready to fight at any moment, if it comes down to it.

Because of me.

I'm the touchstone, the pivot point between them, and dammit, I just want to run far away from this madness.

Another figure steps forward from the circle, and my breath chokes in my throat. *Jesus, am I about to be claimed by yet another wolf?*

But this is an older man with thick gray hair and an even grayer beard, the lines by his eyes thick and deep. He claps his hands and the murmuring falls silent.

"It is not possible for a mate to be claimed by three different wolves," he says in a deep, scratchy voice. "The bond is formed between one male wolf and one female wolf, as it has been since time immemorial."

"Then how do you explain this, Elder Barton?" the turquoise-eyed shifter asks haughtily, motioning to Ridge and the golden-haired man.

"Two of you are mistaken, Trystan," the elder intones, then his gaze shifts to Ridge. "Or lying."

"No one is lying," Ridge says through gritted teeth. "Despite our somewhat colorful pasts, I know neither of these men are liars. And I'm certainly not either."

The man named Trystan huffs but gives a sharp nod. "I'm not accusing anyone of lying. Although those two could be *mistaken*," he adds pointedly, jerking his chin toward Ridge and the blond man.

There's another small burst of muttering among the crowd, but the elder holds up his hand again, effectively silencing them all. He crosses his arms over his flannel shirt and levels his calculating gaze on Ridge.

"You are sure your wolf has claimed this woman?"

Ridge looks at me, his gaze fierce and protective. It's like his amber eyes are made of fire, sparks dancing in their depths. "As sure as I am of my own name."

Warmth blooms inside me as his words settle over me, and against my better judgment, I take a single step toward him. When he sees me move his way, his face softens, shifting his expression back to the man who held me beneath the shower last night as I pieced my mind back together.

"Trystan?" the elder says, turning to the blue-eyed man.

The shifter with chocolate brown hair and confident demeanor nods. "She is mine."

Mine...

Even as I'm straining to fight the urge to reach Ridge, I sway toward this other man, this Trystan. I'm floored by the sudden and immediate response in my body at the sound of his voice.

Ridge growls under his breath, and there's an echoing growl from the golden-haired man behind me.

Oh, fuck. If all three of them are so certain their wolves have claimed me, are they going to have to do something crazy like fight over me? Just the idea sends terror piercing through my heart. I reevaluate the open door, my gaze darting in that direction as I try to decide whether or not I should run.

The elder gives both men a stern glare, but then nods at the blond man and asks, "Archer? Are you positive?"

"Yes, Elder. My wolf is certain this woman is mine."

Mine...

As if in a daze, I swivel on my heel to look at Archer, drawn to meet his eyes. While Ridge and Trystan are both darkly handsome in their own separate ways, Archer is a boy-next-door type, with shimmering blond hair and moss-green eyes. When our gazes meet, he gives me a soft smile that sends a little thrill through me, and I whip around, latching back on to Ridge's gaze as if I've done something wrong.

Through the niggle of panic that's still trying to burst free, I recognize that I'm reacting unconsciously to each man. None of them are willing to back down. They're all certain I'm their "mate," whatever that means. And weirdly enough, I'm drawn to all three of them too.

I can't even pretend to know what's going on here. Obviously, I know the textbook definition of a mate, and I know that for most animals, basic biology drives them to find a good match and propagate their species. I was kept away from the world, but not kept from books. Uncle Clint taught me to read before his treatment of me devolved into nothing but cruelty and neglect, and books became my lifeline in the midst of despair. I even watched some movies on the old TV he kept in the basement until it broke, so I'm not totally ignorant of the world.

But what does it mean for a *shifter* to mate?

I refuse to let myself explore that thought too deeply. So much has been thrown at me in the past two days that I'm confused and in borderline panic mode as it is. The last thing I need to do is add strong emotions to this circus.

The elder catches Ridge's eye, drawing his attention away from me. "I think, Alpha, that in light of recent events, it would be best for us to postpone the rest of this meeting. Do you agree?"

Ridge shakes his head as if to clear it. As if he's reminding himself who he is and where he is. He looks a little dazed, and I'm comforted a bit by the thought that I'm not the only one who's been thrown by this new development.

"Yes." The rugged man makes a circle where he stands, addressing the crowd. "You are all dismissed. Keep lines of communication open and stay vigilant against the witch threat. We will reconvene this summit soon."

Though there's a general air of agreement among the few dozen gathered shifters, I can tell many people aren't amused by the turn. Lawson in particular stands beside me looking as if he's about to make the terrifying transformation into a wolf so he can go for someone's jugular.

"So we're going to ignore the fact that Ridge brought a stranger into our midst?" he snaps at the elder.

The elder looks down his patrician nose at Lawson.

"Calm down, cub. This is none of your concern. The mate bond is a sacred thing, and if that is truly what this is, it overrides our other laws and customs. Even the treaty."

"And the next time you burst into a council meeting where you are not invited, brother, I won't be lenient."

Ridge's words are full of so much controlled fury and power that nearly every shifter in the building backs up a half-step, as if Ridge is the epicenter of a bomb and they've all been hit by the blast.

Lawson growls, but he stalks away without a backward glance, shoving past the people gathered near the door before disappearing from the barn. Only after he's gone do I realize how much his chaotic, aggressive presence was affecting me. My knees go a little weak as a rush of relief floods my body.

I barely move, but Ridge notices the change in me anyway. His gaze snaps back to mine, and he strides toward me, one strong hand wrapping around my good elbow.

"Are you all right?" he asks gently, his strangely-hued eyes searching me as if checking for visible injuries—or *new* ones, anyway.

His gaze lingers on the arm Lawson nearly yanked from its socket, and a little of the pure fury from earlier ignites in his eyes again. I know he saw how roughly the other man treated me, and I get the feeling it's a testament to Ridge's self-control that Lawson is still alive.

I nod, too exhausted and strung out to catalogue all of my injuries. But my knees still feel wobbly. I'm coming down from the adrenaline rush.

"What's going on?" I ask him, my voice barely a whisper. "What are you all talking about? I'm... I'm not a wolf."

12

SABLE

RIDGE GLANCES at Trystan and Archer, who are both watching us with intense expressions.

"I honestly don't know," he murmurs, squeezing my hand as he turns back to me. "But there's something in you that speaks to my wolf. And theirs as well, I guess. We need to find out why."

The elder finishes ushering everyone out and returns to us, his gaze sweeping over me for what seems like the first time. He purses his lips, pity filling his face as he takes in my bedraggled appearance. But I notice a careful sort of distance in his expression too, and I wonder if part of him believes what Lawson said. Does he think I'm a witch?

"I think it's best if we go see Elder Jihoon," he says finally. "Perhaps he can help."

I look to Ridge for an explanation, but he's exchanging glances with Trystan and Archer. Something unspoken passes between all of them, and I bite down hard on my bottom lip as I attempt to decipher some shred of its meaning.

Dammit. I hate this feeling of being outside my depth, or not knowing what the hell is happening.

The panic still simmering beneath my skin wants me to scream and shout and demand answers, but I know, logically, that doing so will just make even more of a case against Ridge for bringing a crazy person into their village. I've been trouble enough for him since the moment he brought me home. I don't want to make his life any harder.

We leave the barn, Ridge still gripping my elbow lightly as if he's laying physical claim to me, and silently head through the village. The barn was already on the outskirts, far from Ridge's little cabin, but we walk farther into the wilderness instead of heading back into the village proper. We pass a few final houses, stretched farther apart than the rest, before the elder veers off from the dirt road and up a weed-covered path to a tiny, corrugated metal cabin that looks as if a stiff wind might knock it over.

The elder's knock makes the whole structure shiver, and we wait in skin-crawling silence for an answer. A cool breeze shifts my hair around my face, and I shudder, pressing tighter to Ridge's side. On my right, Trystan's gaze shifts to us; he presses his lips together, looking angry.

I don't know if he's mad at Ridge or me or this entire situation, but what am I supposed to do? Does he want me to be leaning against *him* like this? I don't know Trystan at all. Or Archer, for that matter. It's weird enough to feel like Ridge is my ally and friend, when all I've done is get his clothes wet in the midst of a panic attack and sleep in his bed.

The door swings open with an audible screech that echoes off the mountains behind the structure. A little old man peers out at us from dark, almond-shaped eyes that I doubt miss anything at all. He's small and wizened with long gray hair bound in a loose bun at the back of his head.

He lifts one graying brow, taking us all in with a sweep of his gaze. "Yes?" His focus lands on me last, and his eyes narrow. "Who is this?"

"This is Sable, Elder Jihoon. Sable..." Ridge turns to me, trailing off with a question in his gaze.

"Sable Maddock," I supply. I can't see any benefit to trying to keep my identity a secret from these people. The situation has spiraled so far out of my control that questions of whether they'll call the cops or alert my uncle seem almost like the least of my worries now.

"We need your help determining whether Sable is a shifter," Ridge continues. "We believe she is, but it would be helpful to know for certain."

"Well, nothing in life is ever certain, Alpha." The little man chuckles. "You know that. But I'll do what I can. Come in, come in."

By the time we've gained entrance to Elder Jihoon's

hut and are scattered around the living room, the first elder —Elder Barton, I deduce from conversation—has caught the older man up on the high drama we seem to have built on the council floor.

Elder Jihoon stares at me for a very long, very uncomfortable moment, his fingers stroking his short, scruffy beard.

"Quite interesting. You know nothing of any of this?" He directs the question at me, leaning forward as if he wants to hear me better.

I jolt, unprepared to be put on the spot like this. Then I swallow and shrug helplessly. "No, sir. I grew up in a small town. I'm not a shifter or a witch. There's nothing special about me."

"I'd hardly say that," Ridge offers with a little smile.

Elder Jihoon stares at me for a long moment, barely seeming to notice that Ridge has spoken. Finally, he gets to his feet and shuffles away, disappearing through the only other open door in the shack. He reappears a moment later carrying two metal rods.

"Stand, please," he says, motioning at me with one of the rods.

I do as he asks, though I'm wary of the tools in his hands. Elder Jihoon is so calm and unassuming, just being in his presence has calmed me after the spectacle in the barn. His peaceful demeanor doesn't exactly make me amenable to being within reach of those metal rods though.

I stiffen and keep my hands loose, ready to bat the things away if they get too close.

Both metal rods are thin and taper to sharp points. Elder Jihoon holds them by wooden handles that are separate from that actual metal and curve downward at a ninety-degree angle. When I glance at Ridge, he just gives me an encouraging nod that isn't really helpful against the terror I'm struggling to hold back.

Elder Jihoon walks around me with the rods pointing straight at my body. He moves slowly, gently lowering and raising the rods from my head to my abdomen as he walks. I watch with a sense of odd detachment as the rods dangle and shift seemingly on their own.

How the hell did I come to be here? Standing in this musty shed, smothered by the scent of a strong, heady incense as a strange old man waves sticks at me and three wolf shifters declare I belong to each of them.

How is this even *real life?*

But if I'm truly honest with myself, I'd rather be here amidst this chaos and insanity than back at Uncle Clint's house worried about whether I'd end the day in blood and pain. This isn't at all what I expected when I threw myself out of his car that night—hell, I'm not sure I expected *anything;* I certainly had no solid plan—but at least I'm still alive.

I stand stock still for so long in the drifting incense smoke that I lose all track of time or self. Is this really happening? Or is it happening to someone else and I'm already dead? Maybe I died at the bottom of the ravine and everything else has been some weird fever dream in the afterlife.

Finally, the old man steps away and lowers his metal sticks.

"The dowsing rods do not lie," he intones. "Though we cannot be sure until she manifests, I do believe there is a wolf inside this woman."

13

SABLE

THE ELDER'S words send a rush of surprise through me, and I blink away some of the daze.

There's a wolf in me?

Looking around at the men who are watching me, I try to work through the detachment I feel. Ridge, Trystan, Archer, even the two elders, these men are all *wolves*.

Wolf shifters, specifically.

Part man, part animal.

I was able to work through the initial shock when Ridge revealed the truth to me while we sat on his bed this morning. It still sounded bat shit crazy, but I saw that man in his living room shift into a wolf. Seeing is believing, right?

But... *me?* I can't even process the possibility. I'm just a girl. A girl with an uncle who's been vicious, cruel... and inhuman.

The thought jogs my brain and shakes away the last of the cobwebs. Could Clint be a shifter, too? Were my parents? They must've been, if I am.

"How?" The word comes out choked and almost too low to be decipherable. "Wouldn't I know? I've... I've never *shifted* in my life."

Elder Jihoon places his metal rods on the table and sits on the couch with the stiff movements of a man with aching joints. He taps his chest with a single arthritic finger. "That's not surprising. Your wolf lives inside you. If a shifter is not raised to embrace the wolf from the beginning, the beast will wait until you are ready before emerging."

Maybe his words are meant to be reassuring, but if they are, they miss the mark. Then again, I'm not sure there's much that *could* reassure me right now.

I sink down to the scratchy couch cushions beside the elder, my head feeling light and airy.

"Why wouldn't my uncle have told me?" I ask, horrified to find my voice still isn't cooperating. The detachment is trying to creep back in, and I'm fighting the urge to rip Elder Jihoon's incense burner off the wall and chuck it out the window. I'm suffocating under the thick smoke as yet another panic attack tries to manifest inside me.

But Ridge is apparently getting a handle on the "Sable is on the verge of disintegrating" mumble. He puts a soft hand on my shoulder, letting its weight rest there without holding on to me. His expression softens as he murmurs, "It's not outside the realm of possibility that your uncle has no pack. Even your parents might not have had a pack."

Archer, who's leaning against the arm of the couch, nods his agreement. "With the way packs have splintered in recent years, we've seen an uptick in lone wolves. Shifters who think they'll be safer alone. So there are plenty of solitary wolves out there."

Trystan scoffs and rolls his eyes. He's the farthest from the couch, standing near the wall by the front door as if he's wary about stepping farther into the elder's house. Despite his obvious disregard for what Archer said, he doesn't elaborate on his disagreement. Whatever history the two have, and whatever the backstory there is to the "lone wolves" they're talking about, I honestly can't fathom adding either to my current list of things to deal with.

"So where do we go from here?" Elder Barton asks, his brow wrinkling. "The girl is a shifter, so obviously she's welcome on our lands. But the mating situation is... problematic."

"Perhaps two of you are mistaken?" Elder Jihoon asks, squinting at the three men.

Too late, he realizes what a Pandora's box he's opened. Arguments and insistences start flying at a volume level way too high for such a small house. I collapse back against the couch cushions and do my best to shut out the sound, closing my eyes. I don't want to sit here and listen to them argue yet again, no matter how "strongly" they "feel the bond." I don't want to watch them hurl insults at one another because they don't believe they can all be mated to one woman.

I didn't ask for *any* of this. All I wanted to do was find a way to be free of Uncle Clint. Somehow, I managed to get myself caught up in a different kind of prison.

"Gentlemen!" Elder Jihoon booms in a voice much stronger than I ever expected out of his mouth. The man is small and lithe, so withered a brisk wind could probably knock him off balance. Yet his boom nearly shakes the walls.

My eyes blink open and I gape at the old man in the sudden silence. He hasn't moved—hasn't even lifted a hand —but all three shifters have stopped speaking over one another. This man is an *elder* for a reason more than just his age, apparently. All the men seem to have great respect for both elders, and so did the people back at the barn. They must carry a special status amongst the pack.

"Ultimately," Elder Jihoon says firmly, "Sable's wolf will be the one to decide which of you she forms her bond with. When her wolf is ready to come out, she will make her choice."

"Is there a way to bring her wolf out?" Trystan asks.

"No, we cannot force her out." Elder Jihoon shakes his head, looking a bit scandalized by the idea. "She will emerge in her own due time. However, putting her somewhere safe and secure with her possible mates could help coax her out. Being alone with you would help the wolf decide."

I'm too tired and my nerves are too frayed to complain, though I'm tired of being talked about as if I'm not even in the room. Do I get a say in this? The Sable that *isn't* a wolf —doesn't her opinion matter?

Because right now, I just want to go curl back up beneath the covers on Ridge's bed and pretend none of this is happening. And I definitely don't want any of them trying to force out a wolf I'm not entirely ready to face. One I'm not sure I even believe exists.

I've spent enough of my life having no say in my fate. I don't want to be at the mercy of *any* man, no matter how sweet he is.

None of those thoughts make it past my numb lips though, so the conversation continues unabated around me.

"Not to mention," Elder Barton says, "it's safer for a new wolf on the verge of bonding to be separated from the rest of the pack. Is there a safe way to achieve that?"

"The mating cabin." Ridge glances around the room. "It's empty right now."

Elder Barton lets out a long, low whistle and shakes his head. "You know I respect your authority as alpha, but I'm not so sure going to a remote mountain cabin is safe for any of us right now. Not given the recent witch activity in the area."

"We wouldn't be alone," Ridge points out, tilting his head in Archer and Trystan's direction. "The three of us can handle trouble."

Elder Jihoon chuckles. "The three of you together, alone, would *be* trouble. You would need a chaperone."

Ridge shrugs. "If we're all three committed to pursuing a bond with Sable, it's our only option."

Straightening from his position on the couch's arm, Archer nods. "Then it's agreed. We'll take her to the cabin and spend time with her there until her wolf emerges and chooses its mate."

"We'll keep her safe," Trystan agrees, though he doesn't make a move to step away from the wall.

Then every gaze in the room turns to me.

I freeze, still slouching in the corner of the couch as if I could sink beneath the cushions and hide. They're looking at me expectantly.

"Um. What?" I ask, my voice small and tinny.

Ridge touches my knee, dipping his head a little to catch my darting gaze. "Do you agree?"

"About going to a remote location with three strange men?" I clarify, hoping they're all smart enough to hear the madness of that statement. If the words don't get them, maybe the note of hysteria in my voice will.

But nobody even blinks.

They're serious.

I don't know what to do. I don't know what any of this means.

I can't deny I'm drawn to them. The way my body reacted of its own accord back in the council's barn shocked the hell out of me. And to be honest, the strange pull I feel toward each of them is the only reason I haven't leapt to my feet and made another run for it.

Something *is* there inside me. Something that senses them. That *knows* them.

But my self-preservation instinct currently has the floor. The longer they stare, unblinking, unmoving, the more the panic finally presses through.

My heart kicks up its pace, and I'm on my feet before I even realize I've thought about standing. I back away from them, even as it occurs to me that I'm backing in the opposite direction from the door.

"Sable?" Ridge's voice is soothing. The same gravelly voice he used last night to soothe my fears, to ask me *what makes it stop?*

It's all too much. Too overwhelming. There's nothing to make it stop.

"No." As my breaths come faster, I shake my head wildly, the whole world seeming to spin out of control around me. "No. I don't want to go."

14

ARCHER

THE LAST THING I expected to find when I came to the council meeting today was a mate. Yet, here I am, watching the woman my wolf has claimed tremble like a leaf in a strong wind and aching to go to her.

I don't though. Not yet.

She's so terrified.

Vulnerable.

I've seen fear like that before. I *know* fear like that.

And I wish like hell I wasn't part of the cause of it.

"I can't do this," she says in a light, soft voice, wrapping her arms around her chest. She's wearing a t-shirt and shorts that are far too big for her—man's clothes, probably Ridge's, and fuck if that doesn't send a hot wave of jealousy rippling through my wolf. "I don't want to do this. I can't be a shifter."

Ridge stands and holds both of his hands out toward

her, palms down like she's a wild pup who needs calming. "Sable, you *are* a wolf. It isn't something you can decide not to be."

She shakes her head, her mussed golden hair flinging about. I can see the whites of her eyes as her gaze darts around the too-small living room. "I'm not a wolf. Just... please. No."

And then she's running. Her sneakers slap against the elder's clean hardwood floors as she launches across the room and through the front door. Trystan doesn't even have a chance to jolt, still holding up the fucking wall as the door slams into him for being in the wrong place at the wrong time.

A surge of emotion flows over me, and I tamp it down, forcing my feet to remain firmly planted. Everything in me wants to follow her and ease her fears. The girl is *terrified*, more so than seems logical, but I'm well aware that fear doesn't always follow logic. Been there, done that.

Ridge moves first, taking two steps toward the door. In the same breath, Trystan straightens and makes a move to follow her outside.

But I throw an arm out, stopping them both. "No."

Both men tense and glare at me, and Ridge snarls, "I'm going after her."

"Somebody has to," Trystan adds, his tone scathing.

"Neither of you are capable of understanding her right now," I say firmly. "Not like me."

I've known Ridge and Trystan for a long time. Almost my entire life, really. That happens when your fathers are the alphas of packs who exist peacefully within a treatise. We grew up together—sort of. I've seen them both do a lot of hot-headed things, and they're both reactionary. They can kindle a temper in two seconds flat.

They don't have the experience I have. They weren't captured and imprisoned by witches as a kid; they weren't mentally and emotionally destroyed by the enemy and then left to figure out how to live again.

I have a unique perspective on trauma they'll never understand.

"Sable needs someone who can understand her," I point out. "I know neither of you want to take your mate by force. Right?"

Ridge looks stricken at the thought, and the tension in his shoulders eases slightly. "No. No, never."

"Of course not," Trystan says, crossing his arms. I can tell he's furious at this whole situation, but I know he means it. All of us take the bond seriously, and an important part of the mate bond is the *willingness* of both parties to enter into it.

Wolves don't mate by force. It's not our way.

I glance at the door then hold up both palms toward them. "I have the best chance at talking to her. Just give me a few minutes. All right?"

I don't wait for an answer. The fact that neither of

them have kicked into a light jog yet tells me they're picking up what I'm putting down. They may be jackasses, but they're not dumb.

As I pass over the threshold, Ridge calls my name and stops me on the elder's front path. "You should know Sable's had trauma in her past. She's been abused."

There's an intense level of rage in his voice, and my own rage rises up to meet it. I kinda thought so. You don't end up with a heavy amount of innate terror like Sable seems to struggle with without something pushing you there. But I hate to have confirmation. I don't know her yet, and I'm not the kind of narcissist to pretend I do, but this means we stand on equal ground, she and I.

I nod at Ridge. "Thanks for the heads up. I'll be careful with her."

Then I leave him standing by the shack, watching me sprint away.

Sable isn't running. I can still scent her on the wind up ahead, and I follow that liquid sunshine smell until I find her standing outside the cabin I know belongs to Ridge.

She's on the sidewalk, shifting her weight back and forth from left foot to right foot, teeth digging into her bottom lip. As I get closer, she doesn't notice me, but she whips around and walks away as if she's come to the realization that Ridge's house is not her home.

I give her space as I follow behind her. It's obvious she didn't grow up with her wolf close to the surface—if she had, I wouldn't be able to tail her like this, unnoticed. She would smell me the minute the breeze took a turn or sense me with that deeply innate predator's intuition.

She stops at the edge of the road where the gravel meets the empty grass that stretches between the village and the forest. Funnily enough, she's facing east. Ten miles that way, and she'd run right onto my father's lands. I'm struck by the thought of her there, standing in my home, taking part in my pack and in my life, and something warm and sweet spreads through my chest.

Longing, I realize.

If my wolf is correct and Sable is my mate, that daydream might be a possibility soon enough.

If she doesn't run away first.

But she's hesitating, doing that shift, left foot, shift, right foot thing again. It doesn't take a genius to see she's unsure about leaving. That gives me hope—and the nudge I need to go to her side.

I don't say anything as I halt at the edge of the gravel next to her. There's a half-foot-deep drop to the grass, and the toes of her sneakers peek over that ledge.

My gaze moves up her legs a little, and my jaw clenches. Her knees are dusty and a little scraped up, probably from the way Lawson was dragging her when he hauled her into the council meeting. But there are other, older wounds on her legs too, scars that curve up and around her calves and thighs.

Who the fuck did this to her?

I want to ask, and if I were Trystan, I might. But the whole reason I volunteered to come after her is because I didn't want her to be traumatized any further. I'm sure poking into her past isn't the way to ease her panic.

So I just allow the silence to lengthen between us for a few moments, letting her breathing even out a little more before I speak.

"Pack life is intense," I say. I don't try to pull my tone or use that ridiculous *slow and low, I'm-talking-to-a-crazy-person* voice Ridge used with her. I use my regular tone, regular pitch, because I'm ninety-nine percent certain she's more likely to respond to a voice that isn't making her feel worse than she already feels.

Sable tucks her hair behind her ear and tosses me a glance that's supposed to look unconcerned, but the deep line between her eyebrows gives away her anxiety. "Yeah, no kidding. Forcible mating isn't on my bucket list."

I rock back on my heels and turn my face into the breeze. "Nah, nobody's going to force you to be their mate. Hell, I won't even keep you from leaving if that's what you want."

She doesn't respond. She doesn't leave, either.

"I get it, though," I go on, taking her silence as an invitation. "I know what it's like to feel like you have no control. Like your entire life is spinning out of control, and you have no way to grab the wheel."

"How would you know?" She finally looks at me—really looks at me with those gray-blue eyes. Something's different about them, a bit more open. There's a spark there that I didn't notice back at the elder's house. Like she shut down a part of herself to deal with the situation.

Fuck. I know what that's like a little *too* well. I feel a fresh wave of anger as I try to imagine what she might've been through. If the culprit was in front of me right now, I'd rip his damn heart out and eat it.

I go for candor. What do I have to lose? "Have you heard about the never-ending battle between witches and shifters?"

She makes a little noise in her throat that's almost a laugh. "A little. I don't really understand it. I didn't even know shifters were real two days ago. Or witches either. And I don't know why witches hate shifters."

"Well, that puts you in good company." I chuckle humorlessly. "We don't really get it either. Basically, witches believe only witches should have access to magic. But magic is what allows shifters to shift. We're physically powered by the same phenomena that gives them their powers."

Sable's brow wrinkles as she processes that bit of intel. She's adorable, almost child-like in the way she takes in information. I can almost see her working out the pieces of the puzzle, thinking back over recent conversations until she has a bigger picture. "Seems like you should be allies then."

I laugh. "You would think. Almost like we're family."

A sharp pang tugs in my chest at the thought, and I rub it away. I've had control of my anxiety for years, but baring old wounds threatens my tenuous hold. I don't want to scare her off with the full details of what the witches did to me. But more than that, I don't want to re-open the deep wounds in myself by dredging up all those old emotions, either. It's a dangerous tightrope to walk.

"But you're not?" Sable regards me with serious eyes.

"No. We aren't." I shake my head. "They hate us. For years, they've attacked our kind any way they can. We have protections in place, but when they manage to slip past them, they have only one goal—to destroy shifters. They... hurt me. When I was young. For the longest time, I couldn't sleep without fear. I couldn't walk down the street without worrying they'd come back for me. I couldn't roam the woods or hunt. They took a piece of *myself* away from me."

"That's horrible."

She's watching me, her expression enigmatic, but despite the lack of visible emotion, I can tell she's really listening.

"It's hard to know who to trust," I say, looking away from her and out over the darkening forest. I knew that eye contact, and people who appear to be looking much too deeply into your soul, can inspire panic. "In a world where people you thought you could count on are the ones who hurt you, trust is hard to come by."

Sable makes a humming noise, almost as if she's trying to convince herself to believe me, to trust me, but she can't quite do it.

I get that.

"I can guarantee you something," I add carefully, and her eyelids flicker slightly.

"What?"

I turn toward her so that our gazes can meet. Then I put my hands out, palms up, showing her I'm holding nothing.

Hiding nothing.

That I'm not a threat.

"There's nowhere in this world where you'll be safer than with me, Trystan, and Ridge. We'll keep you safe, Sable. We'll protect you with our lives from whoever hurt you in the past. And we'll guide you until your wolf comes out."

15

SABLE

ARCHER'S GOLDEN, boy-next-door good looks are even more devastating in the oranges and purples of sunset. I have to work hard to focus on his words and not get lost in his brilliant green eyes that remind me of fresh cut grass. He's taller than Ridge, though not by much, but his presence isn't as imposing. He doesn't loom like the other wolves. He doesn't wear his beast as close to the surface.

Despite everything that's happened, I'm drawn to him. It's a stupid thing, really. I shouldn't be drawn to him. I should be drawn to those damn woods and getting the hell away from this mess before I'm too deep to get out. But something about the weight in his voice tells me he's not lying. He's not feigning empathy just to keep me from leaping off this ledge and racing away into the sunset.

Archer's been through some things. Some really heavy things. The same kinds of things I have.

They... hurt me. When I was young.

I can't help but wonder at his story. What did the witches do to him that made it so easy for him to relate to what I've been through? How is it he really seems to understand how I feel? I hate to think someone took this kind, beautiful man as a child and hurt him the way I've been hurt. I hate to think of anybody going through the things I've gone through.

Even so, I want to know Archer's story. I want to know all about him, and I almost ask him to keep talking. I'll stand on this ledge for as many hours as it takes to learn about him.

You don't have the luxury of getting to know someone, I remind myself, reaching for the protective walls around my heart. I pull them close and shove them into place to keep him out. Allowing someone into my heart—or even into my head—isn't an option. When you let people in, that's when they can hurt you the most.

"Sable?"

My name on his lips jolts me from my dark thoughts. I'm already looking at his face, but my vision went unfocused while he spoke. I realize now he must have finished talking without me even noticing, and I was left staring at him like a freaking weirdo. I lock gazes with him and make a sound that I hope indicates I was, in fact, hanging onto his every word.

"I hope you'll come with us," he says. "Let us help you."

There's nothing in his tone to indicate I've irritated him with my inattention, which is a relief. I don't know him, and I know that means I obviously shouldn't care what he thinks, but I still don't want to hurt his feelings. I didn't ignore what he was saying on purpose.

My mind just hasn't stopped reeling. It's hard to collect my thoughts and keep them in any kind of order for more than a few minutes.

I'm determined to no longer be a doormat. If I said no right here, right now, he'd take it for the final answer and let me go. Something about him promises me he would. I have the power and the ability to say *no*, more than I ever have in my entire life. But... I don't want to say it.

I kind of want to say yes.

So I convince myself I'm doing it for his benefit. I don't want him to think I hate him. I don't want to walk away from Ridge without telling him thank you. What kind of person would that make me?

And honestly, I don't know where on earth I would go if I don't stay here. The path of least resistance is to stick around and see where this circus leads me.

"Okay," I agree. "I'll stay."

Archer's smile transforms his face, making him even more handsome, as if the sun itself is shining from behind his eyes. "Great. I'm glad, Sable. I promise you won't regret it."

My heart does a confused little flip. Partly because I'm not certain I *won't* regret this decision. But also because his smile is affecting me in ways I don't really understand. I'm not used to men drawing out this kind of reaction in me. Nobody has ever had this effect on me, and it scares me.

The panic rears up like it always does, but I breathe through it.

I will *not* shut down.

We walk silently back down the road. Archer stays at my side, but he gives me an excessive amount of personal space that helps keep the panic at bay. He shoves his hands in his pockets, and he doesn't try to make small talk. I appreciate that, too, considering Ridge and Trystan are watching us come toward them.

Both men are standing on the lawn behind Ridge's house. I hate to think they stood there and watched me and Archer talking, but I'm sure that's what they did. Their gazes all seem to have some kind of magnetic pull toward me, finding me unerringly anytime I'm near them.

I don't know if I believe in this "mate bond" thing they're all talking about, but it's hard to deny that there's *something* between us. Something that crackles in the air like an invisible electric charge.

Oh my God. This is insane.

These three men each feel they have a claim to me, and

I've agreed to give them a chance to prove it. Jesus. What the hell am I thinking?

Trystan watches me approach with a hint of desire in his gaze, but Ridge is staring at me as if searching for any new injuries. He waits until I meet his gaze before he asks, "You okay?"

I nod. "As good as I can be."

Ridge nods in return. He probably didn't expect anything less from the crazy girl he dragged in from the woods like a half-drowned kitten. Turning to Archer, he says, "Barton will alert the council of our imminent absence, and the reason why."

When he tosses a subtle glance at me, I flush. All this focus on me makes me want to sink into the ground and disappear.

"And rescheduling the meeting?" Archer asks.

Ridge shakes his head. "We'll discuss a more cohesive defense against the witches at the next summit. In the meantime, the packs will continue to defend themselves as they have been."

Trystan claps Ridge on the shoulder. "Well then. Let me go talk to my pack mates before they head back."

"I should do the same," Archer says as the brown-haired wolf brushes past him. "We'll meet you back here in fifteen."

As the two stride off back in the direction of the council house, where I can see a group of people still milling about outside, Ridge offers me his hand. I'm too distracted to decline, and I slide my smaller hand into his. His palm is warm and calloused, and the feel of his skin against mine sends little tingles all the way up my arm to my heart. Without a word, he leads me through the back door into the house.

"Will you be all right on your own for a few minutes?" he asks. "I've got to pack up."

"Yeah."

The word comes out with more strength than I expected, but it still takes great force of will to make myself let go of his hand. My skin feels too cold immediately, and I clasp my own hands together to try to combat the feeling of emptiness.

Maybe Ridge notices my reaction, or maybe it's because he feels something similar. But he seems reluctant to leave, hesitating for a long moment before nodding and moving across the room.

I sit on the edge of the couch as Ridge disappears into the bedroom. I can hear him rifling through drawers and shoving hangers around in his closet. When he returns a few minutes later, he's hauling two large satchels and a smaller one, and he tosses them down by the front door. I remain where I am, out of his way and feeling as if I don't belong here. He gathers more supplies—flashlights, tools, and some nonperishable items from the kitchen, depositing them in the bags.

What the hell am I doing? The mantra repeats over and over in my head.

The situation seems too real now as I watch him pack basic necessities for the group of us. I've agreed to go to a cabin in a remote location with three men I don't know. On what planet is that a safe or smart idea?

Maybe the planet where men can be wolves and witches exist? The small voice in my head sounds almost amused, and I bite my lip to stifle the slightly crazed smile that threatens.

As he zips up the two large packs, Ridge remarks, "This smaller bag is yours. My friend Amora donated some clothes and necessities for you. She's probably a bit bigger than you, but they should work."

I nod, wondering who Amora is. Is "friend" just a euphemism? Is Amora his girlfriend?

The idea that he might belong to someone else makes me crazy with an unreasonable sort of jealousy, and I bite back any desire to question him about her. I'm fragile enough without adding excess fuel to the fire.

Leaving the bags by the door, Ridge leaves the room one more time. When he comes back, he's got a small bottle and a few white pieces of gauze in his hands. He approaches me with smooth, even steps, as if wanting to make sure he doesn't scare me.

He doesn't though.

He's broad and imposing, but for some reason I'm not

afraid of him, even if his presence always seems to take up the whole room.

When he reaches me, he kneels on the hardwood floor in front of me, grimacing slightly as he takes in the sight of my scraped and dirty knees. His gaze flicks up to meet mine. "I'll clean and disinfect these, okay?"

I nod, unable to look away from the sight of this massive man kneeling before me.

Working quickly, he dabs some disinfectant on one of the gauze pads before brushing the pad over my knee. I hiss at the sting, and he freezes immediately, clenching his jaw as if it hurts him to.

He looks up at me again. "You all right?"

"Yeah." I swallow. "It just stings a little. I've felt worse."

I shouldn't have said that. His gaze drops to the scars crisscrossing my bare legs beneath the oversized shorts, and he clenches the gauze pad so tightly that little drops of disinfectant drip from the bottom of his closed fist.

His tension makes my skin prickle, so to distract him, I ask, "Is he really your brother? Lawson?"

The anger in his expression doesn't go away, but it morphs into a new kind as he shakes his head with a grunt. "Yes. Really. Unfortunately."

"He's kind of an asshole."

I feel safe saying this, considering I'm pretty sure

Ridge already knows it. And he proves me right when he laughs humorlessly.

"Yes. That he is." His features soften a little as he starts swiping gently at my skin with the wet pad again. "I'm sorry for what he did. He'll pay for it, I promise you that. And I won't let him touch you ever again."

The truth in his words sends a little shiver up my spine —a mixture of fear and something else I can't quite name. He means it.

I don't know how to respond to that, so I let silence fall between us as he continues cleaning up the little scrapes on my knees. His big hands are surprisingly careful as he dabs the disinfectant over each little tear in my skin.

When he's done, he sets everything on the coffee table beside the couch before looking up at me, his big palms resting on my thighs just above the knee. He gives a soft squeeze, and I feel one corner of my lips tilt up into a smile.

"Thank you," I murmur.

"Of course."

He gazes up at me for another long moment before he finally moves. Sitting beside me on the cushions, he slides a finger beneath my chin and tilts my face up toward his.

"You don't have to do this." His gruff voice is gentle, and his gaze sweeps my face as if he can see right through me.

Hell, maybe he can. From the moment I woke up here, he's been able to sense my fear, my panic, and calm me down. Now, I'm sure he can clearly sense my thoughts and just how stressed I am over this extremely odd situation. Like every other action he's taken in my presence, his statement is one more way in which he seems determined to protect me.

Warmth unfurls inside me, and I lean into his touch. His protection feels like a force-field, cutting me off from the storm brewing inside me. I focus on the heat of his finger on my chin, way too aware of his closeness and his breath not far from my lips.

I could take him up on this offer. Back out now. But there's something in me that can't do it. Instead of my usual instinctual need to flee, I want to stay right here forever with his finger on my skin and his warmth radiating over me. As long as he's there to comfort me, I'll be all right.

"Thank you. But I'm going," I say resolutely. "I—I want to."

The tension in his forehead melts away, and the corners of his lips turn up, making his ruggedly handsome face even more beautiful. "Good. I'm glad."

We stare at one another for so long that I feel like I'm going to drown in his eyes. When his gaze drops to my lips, my stomach flutters, and the warmth inside me unfurls further.

He brushes his thumb over the line of my jaw, making

every nerve ending in my body sing. A sound escapes me, and I sway toward him a fraction of an inch, lost in him.

Entranced by him.

Drowning in the strange connection I can neither understand nor deny.

"I'm so glad I found you that night, Sable," Ridge murmurs. "I wish I'd found you long before then."

I think I know what he means, even without him saying it. He wishes he'd known me long enough to keep the bad things in my life from hurting me. To keep me safe.

I could tell him that he would've had to have met me when I was a child for that to be possible, but I don't want to ruin the sweetness of this moment. I don't want him to stop looking at me the way he is, with hunger and tenderness all rolled into one.

My body shifts toward him a little more, and Ridge mirrors the movement, closing the space between us...

The front door bangs open.

I jolt, leaping nearly half a foot off the couch as I flash back to the day Lawson and his cronies burst into this same room. Luckily, no raging bullies enter. Just Trystan and Archer, who I *think* aren't bullies. At least, I hope they don't turn out to be, though I guess right now anything is possible.

Trystan pauses just inside the door, his gaze hardening as he surveys the scene they just walked in on—Ridge and me sitting so close together we're sharing the same air, with his hand still touching my face.

"Are we interrupting?" Trystan drawls, his voice dark. Archer peers over his shoulder at us, and a muscle tenses in his jaw.

I quickly scoot away from Ridge before this turns into a dog fight. I've built a kind of... friendship, I guess, with Ridge. But I can't forget that these other two shifters are absolutely certain I'm their mate. I really don't want to have to referee three territorial men. I'm not equipped for that level of violence.

Ridge unfolds from the couch, turning back into the imposing shifter I've come to recognize.

"No. You aren't interrupting." He snatches a pack off the floor near Trystan's feet. "Grab a bag," he adds, then shoves past the two wolves on his way out the front door.

Trystan glares after him while Archer grabs the other bag. Then they both turn to me and wait, watching as I pick up the smaller pack with my hand-me-downs from Ridge's maybe girlfriend. I hike it higher on my shoulder and skirt past them out the door, giving myself a wide berth from their imposing presences.

Ridge is in the front yard waiting in just his boxer shorts, jamming his shirt and pants into his satchel as I appear. My steps falter on the front walk as my gaze roams over the play of muscles across his back.

He glances over his shoulder, giving me a view of his

profile in the evening sunlight. "It's a hike to the cabin. We'll have to shift and run to make it by nightfall. Since you can't shift yet, you're going to have to ride me."

"R-ride you?" I gape at him. Surely that's *not* what he just said.

Ridge grins wolfishly and turns around to face me. His front is even more delicious than his back, and my mouth goes dry as I try to swallow. "Don't worry. It's like riding a bike."

"Somehow I doubt that."

He laughs, seeming amused by my sassy reply. I blink, caught off guard a little. Uncle Clint never found it the least bit amusing when I talked back to him.

As Trystan and Archer join us, shedding their own clothes, Ridge's body begins to shudder and change. I see it now that Archer has told me—how the shift is powered by magic. For a moment, Ridge's body seems to be swallowed up by blackness, and then in the next moment, he's standing on four furry legs with his boxer shorts in pieces at his feet.

The change steals over my other two companions next. I clutch the strap of my satchel, gripping the leather tightly as I try to resist the urge to rub my eyes in cartoonish disbelief. I've seen this once before, in Ridge's living room, but I was caught so off-guard then that I barely processed it. Observing the change when I'm in a more coherent state of mind leaves me nearly breathless with wonder.

The shift only lasts a few seconds before I'm facing three of the largest creatures I've ever seen.

Ridge's fur is a light brown, almost auburn in the dying sunlight, with his belly and legs a lighter tan. His eyes are still the same honey color, and I recognize a sharp, *human* intelligence behind them—which means they don't fully lose themselves in the transformation. Trystan is slightly taller than Ridge with deep chocolate brown fur all over and turquoise eyes, while Archer's wolf has golden fur on his back and a white underside. Like the others, his green eyes are still the same, and they even look compassionate as he cocks his head at me, sensing my roiling emotions.

As Trystan and Archer nudge through the straps on their packs and manipulate the bags onto their backs, I cross to Ridge and try not to give in to my fear.

When I stand before him, his head reaches past my shoulders, even with him on four legs and me on two. He's the size of a small pony, powerfully built and rippling with muscle beneath his thick fur. I put a hand on his side and trail my fingers over him, surprised by how wiry and scruffy his fur is, when he looks so soft.

It takes a couple tries, and some kneeling on his part, for me to scramble onto his broad shoulders. My own bag on my back throws me off until I get it settled directly behind me and find my balance on Ridge's body. He snuffs at me, tossing me a gaze over his shoulder. Apparently, we won't be able to talk while he's in wolf form.

"I'm ready," I tell him, my heart thudding hard in my chest.

He sets into motion, and I dig the fingers of both hands into his fur, clinging to him for dear life. God, how embarrassing would it be if I fell off like a six-year-old at a sideshow pony ride?

After a few steps, I'm able to catch up with the rhythm of his trot. I keep my hands fisted in his fur and my legs tucked around his barrel chest. I'm even kind of enjoying it with the wind picking up in my hair and that snow-and-pine scent drifting from the mountains ahead.

But my good mood is soured when I realize we aren't leaving without an audience.

Lawson stands beneath the shadows of a front porch as we pass through the outskirts of the village, watching us leave with hard, narrowed eyes.

It's been a while since I last ran—the full-out sprint of a wolf with a mission or a wolf at play, sprinting through the mountains as if every hill is a racetrack.

It's a freeing kind of run, cosmic and powerful.

When I'm on patrol, I keep my steps measured and even. It's too easy to let the landscape slide by without seeing potential threats if you don't stop and smell the fucking roses, as my father used to say.

My paws thud against the ground and the cool mountain wind whips past my ears. Archer and Trystan flank me, their keen gazes aware of our surroundings even as the trees and rock flash by at lightning speed. If I had to be alone in the wilderness for any indefinite period of time, I have to admit, these two men aren't the worst backup a wolf could ask for. They're both strong and smart. Trystan's attitude problem makes me want to gut him with my bare claws sometimes, and Archer bears more pain than I think he realizes he lets on to the world. Between his abduction as a cub and his father's drawn-out march toward death, he's had a hell of a lot to deal with.

But they're good wolves.

I worried at first that Sable wouldn't be able to handle the speed, but once she found her balance on my back, she was a natural. Her hands are wrapped firmly in my thick fur, and her legs are clamped hard around my chest. She's so small and light I think I could carry her forever. I can feel every inch of her gorgeous, supple body pressed against me, but it's her breath on my neck, ruffling my fur, that drives me crazy.

Amora surprised me when she found me outside the elder's house after Sable rushed off and shoved a backpack into my arms. "For your girl," she said with a shrug. "She can't wear your clothes forever."

"I like her in my clothes," I pointed out.

Amora bared her teeth at me. "Women like their *own* clothes. It's a gift. Say thank you and take it."

"Thank you," I said honestly, then I raised an eyebrow at her. "You're surprisingly nonchalant about all of this."

"Why not? You're crazy enough for the both of us." She grinned at me before growing serious. "We don't have any control over the mating bond. You know it as well as I do."

She was right—we're both well aware.

For the longest time, the pack expected the two of us to imprint on one another and form a mating bond. When it never happened, we settled into our friendship comfortably and moved on with our lives, even as the elders bemoaned the situation. Amora is well-respected among the pack, and a mate-bond between us would've made perfect sense on paper. Plus, an alpha without a mate is a loose cannon, if you listen to all the old guys bitch.

"Anything I should do while you're gone?" Amora asked. "I know the elders will run things in your stead, but anything they can't handle?"

"Yeah. Keep an eye on Lawson," I told her. "I don't trust him."

She gave me a perfunctory nod, her green eyes darkening. "You and me both."

Even now with the wind in my fur and Sable on my back, I can't stop thinking that leaving the pack right now is a huge fucking mistake. Lawson's been waiting for his moment, and if he decides to do something stupid, the elders won't stand in his way. And they shouldn't have to. It's not their job to quell unruly members of the pack.

It's mine.

I can only hope Amora will keep a sharp eye out for any threat he poses. Because I have no choice. The mating bond is our most sacred tradition, and we have to honor it. All of us—me, Trystan, and Archer. We have to figure out who belongs with Sable and let that bond forge. For the good of our packs and the continuation of our race.

God, what a fucking nightmare. Three of us and one of her. Regardless of tradition and honor and what's good for the pack, the thought of one of them touching her makes my blood boil.

Having her this close to me is like pouring gasoline on a dying fire. Nothing separates us but my fur and the thin shorts and t-shirt of mine that still cover her body. The powerful way her thighs grip my shoulders inflame every instinct in me, and I'm fucking mindless with the need to shift back and claim her. Press her into the dirt right here on the side of the goddamned mountain and fill every inch of the sweetness between her legs with my cock.

But I don't.

Because I shouldn't.

Because when—*if*—Sable ever truly becomes mine, she'll deserve the best I can give her. Not some desperate fuck by the side of the road.

Because as badly as I want her body, I want her soul more. I want her heart.

And it will take time to earn that.

So I focus on our surroundings like the damn alpha I'm supposed to be. We need to stay alert and on guard so we don't get caught unawares by witches. Trystan and Archer are doing a damn fine job of it, while I'm in the middle with a raging metaphorical hard-on, imagining Sable naked in the dust.

Way to prove yourself fucking worthy of her, I admonish myself.

We follow the branded trees along our route, knowing that we're somewhat safer if we remain within their boundaries. All three packs worked together on these routes of safe passage—the sigils burned into the trees keep the witches away and make it safer for us to travel over land. Though, to be fair, the last few violent deaths had happened well within our marked boundaries.

The witches were getting craftier, and that reminder fills me with guilt. Our meeting today should have been the first step in ensuring further safety for our people. But it was completely fucked by Lawson dragging Sable in like he had some kind of personal vendetta against her.

That fucking ass-hat. The moment I saw him manhandle her into the center of the room, every cell in my body cried for his total annihilation. The only thing that held me back was the look in Sable's eyes.

I didn't want her to ever look at me like that. With such fear. With such pure, abject terror.

And she would have, if I'd ripped my brother limb from limb right in front of her.

The sun is fully gone when we come to a steady halt outside the mating cabin. We're about sixty miles from the North Pack village but still within shifter territory. We're at the base of a mountain, deep within a thickly wooded area so far off the beaten path that there's not a chance in hell anything could find us here, human or otherwise.

Safe. For now.

Sable slips off my back, her body sliding over mine like silk. I shudder as she rubs over me, her fingers trailing in my fur, and I know she feels the shiver wrack my body. I can smell arousal in her body too. Faint, but there. She knows—without knowing *how* she knows— exactly what I'm feeling. She hits the ground, knees nearly buckling, and digs her fingers into my fur to hold herself upright.

I call on my magic to shift back before she can let go of me. I want to feel her fingers on my bare skin. I want it so fucking bad it's all I can think about, and I'm damn lucky I don't shift back to human with a rock hard dick.

The magic fades, and Sable's hands are on my bare chest, her satin fingers resting near my nipples.

Her eyes widen and her gaze drops between us to my nakedness. I realize too late that I probably should have warned her. All of us are so used to seeing our pack mates naked, it's just a regular part of life. Something tells me Sable's never seen a man's cock before.

And her gaze on mine pulses blood directly to that body part.

She backs away quickly, clutching at the straps on her backpack as her eyes dart away. But Trystan and Archer have shifted back too, so when she turns her head she gets an eyeful of them instead.

She lets out a small squeak and a red hot flush rises up her pale neck, painting her cheeks. Then she whirls on her heel and sprints toward the cabin, racing inside as if she can't get away from the three naked dudes fast enough.

I'm not entirely comfortable with her running into the cabin alone before one of us checks it for wild animals or interlopers, but she doesn't immediately scream bloody murder, so I consider that proof the cabin is safe. I'll do a more thorough check in a second, but first...

I step ahead of Trystan and Archer to stop them before they go inside.

"We need to make something clear," I say, pitching my voice low so Sable doesn't accidentally hear me.

Trystan crosses his arms, his face turning to stone. "What? You trying to make some kind of 'I found her first' claim? Tell that to my wolf. We each have an equal chance here, fuckface."

I clench my fists against the urge to break his stupid nose. "No, jackass. About Sable's state of mind."

"She's been hurt badly before. Physically and emotionally. I can tell." Archer speaks up, adjusting his pack on his shoulders.

"She has. Anyone with eyes can see she's traumatized." I glance toward the cabin, seeing the network of scars on Sable's pale flesh in my mind's eye. "I don't know the details, but we gotta be gentle with her. She's not used to this. *Any* of it. Nobody push her beyond what she can handle."

Archer nods. "It's more important that we respect her trauma than it is to urge her wolf to come out. We have to let her do this at her own pace."

Trystan scoffs. "Thank you, Doctor Phil."

I jam a finger into the man's broad chest. "Play. Fucking. Nice. This is your only warning. If you so much as give her a nightmare, I'll eat your entrails and feed the rest to the vultures. Got it?"

Trystan's jaw clenches so tight I think he might break a few teeth off. But he finally nods, taking a step away from my finger. His eyes burn with annoyance as he glares at me, but his expression softens as he glances toward the small cabin. A hint of worry crosses his face, and he nods.

"Yeah. I got it."

17

SABLE

I PRESS my forehead to the wall just inside the front door, letting all the weight of my body ooze against the cool wooden planks. My knees damn sure can't hold me up anymore.

The cabin is dim and musty, as if the windows haven't been opened for months. I'm in what seems to be a living room area, although I didn't take much time to look at it when I walked in.

My skin is flushed and hot as if I have a fever, and I consider going to see if there's a freezer I can shove my head in. Pressing my hands to my cheeks, I focus on taking a couple of deep breaths and calming the fluttering in my stomach.

I can't seem to catch my breath, and I feel hot and achy all over in a way I've never experienced before. I can't get the sight of Ridge's body out of my mind. Every single part of him is etched in my memory, and the feeling curling between my legs begs me to keep replaying that memory over and over.

Even when I tried to look away, to *drag* my gaze away from him... there were Trystan and Archer, both just as magnificent and just as damn naked.

The one true string of luck I had in my miserable life was that my uncle never abused me sexually. Clint liked the power of hurting me physically—lording his strength over me with pain, keeping me quiet and pliant with threats of knives and lashes and "accidents." Even his gross friends who came over every once in a while never hurt me like that. There was one man who got creepy with me a few times, and I lived in absolute terror that he might one day lose control and try to...

But he didn't.

I know *about* sex, but I've never done it before. I've never even kissed anyone, and everything I know about the subject was gleaned from books and movies and unpleasant conversations between my uncle and his buddies that I wish I hadn't heard.

But this?

I don't know anything about this. I'm not familiar with the kind of need that seeps through my bones and makes every nerve-ending seem to come alive. So this aching, throbbing heat between my legs is as newly bizarre as it is decadent.

Jesus, the three of them were as perfect as pictures I've seen of Greek god statues. Every muscle might as well have been chiseled out of stone with an eye for perfection. Every curve of their bodies were powerful and strong, the way their waists tapered into their hips and their muscular legs...

Just recalling the image of the three of them standing together completely naked is turning me into a puddle of raw, sparking lust.

Okay. Breathe, I tell myself, dragging in two long, steady breaths and letting them out with the same care. *Get a grip, Sable. You're acting ridiculous. It's just men's bodies. Obviously, nudity isn't a big deal to shifters.*

Before I can get a handle on my emotions, the door opens and all three shifters pile into the small living room. I straighten and clutch my pack against my chest as if it might provide a real barrier between us.

Ridge reaches past Archer and finds the light switch on the wall. A bare bulb illuminates high over my head, casting light onto the three still naked men in front of me. I gape at them, too astonished to even recognize that a cabin in the middle of nowhere is clearly equipped with electricity. I guess mating pairs wanted to be able to see each other.

Naked.

Obviously.

Jesus, take the wheel.

Trystan steps ahead of the other two and comes close to me. A cocky grin settles over his face and he gently takes my pack from my numb hands, tossing it over his own shoulder. It takes every ounce of my willpower to not look down. He's so close I can smell his skin—something earthy, like incense, something darker than Ridge's clear pine scent.

He's the most arrogant of them, I think. The way he continues to stand there, holding my bag as if he's doing me a favor, that crooked grin on his face like he *knows* I want to look at his body. Like he knows he's a damn fine sight to see, and he wants me to partake.

I refuse to give in. No matter how badly I want to.

A hand clamps down onto Trystan's shoulder, and Ridge rounds on him with a glare. "Did you forget already? Come on. Let's get dressed."

As the three men move off down the hallway, I sink against the wooden wall and struggle to get breath back into my lungs. Their presences are insanely strong, as if I can drink in their essence just by being in the same room with them.

When I finally get my wits back, and I've given them ample time to cover up, I follow them down the hall. Since Trystan took my bag, I need to retrieve it from him in order to change out of Ridge's dirty clothes. I'm covered in the dirt and dust that was kicked up during our run.

As luck would have it, all three men are dressed when I find them in the bedroom.

The *only* bedroom.

This cabin is a lot smaller than Ridge's house, and although it looks like there's a small kitchen as well as the living room, there are definitely no more bedrooms.

"Um, one bed?" I ask, tentatively moving into the room. Trystan has laid my bag on the bed atop the colorful quilt, and I squeeze around Archer to get to it.

Ridge tugs the hem of his shirt down and replies, "We'll sleep in the living room. You can have the bed."

Thank goodness for small mercies. I can't even imagine trying to sleep next to all that... man.

Trystan makes a noise that sounds suspiciously like distaste, but Ridge shoves him toward the door. "Let's make sure the cabin is stocked."

As Archer passes me, he offers me a small, shy smile. "Take your time. We'll be waiting for you when you're ready."

I spend an inordinately long time beneath a cold shower, wondering where the water came from this deep in the wild, and if the water could go even colder to wash away the desire that still burns through me with a vengeance.

Ridge's friend Amora gave me a bag full of clothes, including comfy sweats and nightshirts. Right now, baggy cotton pants thick enough to hide all my curves seem like the safest bet, and I top them off with a long-sleeved nightshirt that hangs off me like a potato sack. I know I probably look ridiculous, but the less skin I have showing in their presence, the better.

For all of us.

The more I have to take off, the more likely I won't give in to the insane desire to press my bare skin against theirs the way my palms pressed against Ridge's chest.

When I walk into the small kitchen at the back of the house, my three companions are seated at a wooden table barely large enough for them with an array of food waiting. It's more than I saw Ridge pack in one of the bags, which I guess isn't that surprising. I recall him saying something about the cabin being stocked.

It appears to be a do-it-yourself sandwich assembly line. Though each man has an open soda sitting before them, none of them have helped themselves to the food yet. I can't help but feel a little touched that they waited for me.

"Ladies first," Trystan teases, motioning to the only empty chair.

After I pile my bread with cold cuts, cheese, and condiments, the guys dive in with gusto. My sandwich looks like a single bite compared to the towering monstrosities they make, and it occurs to me it probably takes a *lot* of fuel to power a shifter's metabolism.

Spurred by the thought, I ask, "Do you guys have to eat more than regular people?"

It doesn't occur to me until after the question is out of my mouth that it might be a little too intimate. Though we are in what amounts to a private sex cabin in the woods, so no question is likely off the table.

"We do." Archer teeth flash white as he smiles. "Our bodies run hotter and faster, so we need more fuel than the average human."

Their bodies certainly do run hotter, I can't deny that. My cheeks flush again as I try desperately not to conjure up images of them without any clothes. It's not really working, so I blurt out another question to distract myself.

"I never knew shifters even existed, but to be honest, my life was kinda... Well, I was shielded from a lot. Does the world know about you at all?"

Ridge sets his soda can down on the table with a clank. "No. They can't know. For good reason."

"What reason is that?"

Trystan shoves his hand into the bag of chips in the center of the table as he replies. "Shifters have existed for thousands of years. We learned early on that if humans find out about us, they inevitably try to hunt us to extinction."

I gasp, horrified. "*Hunt* you?"

Ridge shoots a look of irritation at Trystan before

turning to me. "Humans have a tendency to be fearful of things they can't explain. Magic, shifters, the lot of it."

"And where humans are fearful, there follows destruction," Archer murmurs with a shake of his head.

Trystan snorts. "Ha. Humans are nothing compared to witches. Humans may hunt us because they fear us. Witches hunt us because they hate us."

That statement brings forth a whole new slew of questions. I have a million to ask—if I'm stuck with these men for an indefinite amount of time, I would do well to learn about them and their culture. The good news is, they seem to like hearing me talk. Already, Ridge is looking at me expectantly, as if waiting for my next query.

"Archer told me a little bit about the witch problem. But could you tell me more?" I ask. "Why do they hate you *so* much?"

Trystan slouches in his chair, cradling his soda against his abdomen. "Don't let the word fool you. *Witches* can be women *and* men. They use magic. To them, we're an aberration."

"Because you use magic to shift," I say to clarify what I gleaned from Archer.

"Right." Trystan nods, a grin touching his lips. "We're using something that belongs to them—that they believe should *only* belong to them. So in their minds, we're something wrong or worthless that shouldn't exist."

His words hit me harder than I was prepared for, and I

freeze, playing them over in my head.

We're something wrong or worthless that shouldn't exist.

I realize with heart-wrenching clarity that this kind of belief—viewing someone as inherently worthless—was exactly what my uncle did to me.

My heart clutches, and it feels like my whole chest has seized up. I can't breathe. I can't speak.

As if a cold hand has reached out from my past and dragged me back, I feel myself falling away from the small, comfortable kitchen, hurtling into dark memories of a place I know all too well.

Clint's house.

My childhood house.

The house of my nightmares.

Uncle Clint stands over me, a cigarette in his hand and a sneer on his ugly, twisted face. I'm cowering against the wall, a glass of water spilled on the floor at my feet. He kicked me in the back as I passed him. I was carrying a glass of water, and I spilled it, and he backhanded me into the wall.

Clint puts his cigarette to his lips and sucks in a lungful of smoke that won't kill him nearly fast enough to save my life. Then his hand darts out and he puts the butt out on my neck. Hot, searing pain lashes over my nerve-endings, and I think I smell burning flesh. On top of the throbbing in my back and head.

"You're a waste of fucking space. A waste of the goddamn food I feed you," he growls, tossing the spent cigarette in my face. "Stupid, worthless girl."

I flinch backward, and as I do, I fall into another memory.

Uncle Clint slips his pocketknife from his jeans and flicks the blade open in a practiced snick. He's holding a short glass of straight whiskey in his other hand, and his eyes have the shiny, distanced look I recognize as the early stages of drunkenness.

I came into the living room to fill his glass because he told me to. Now I'm standing here beside his recliner, staring at the glint of steel in the flickering blue light of the television.

He slashes out at me, the blade cutting into my arm. I recoil, my heart hammering against my rib cage as blood wells on my skin.

"Fucking waste of oxygen," he mutters. "You'll never amount to shit."

The memories keep coming like a bad movie playing in my head, an overwhelming, never-ending horror story that I lived day in and day out for far too long. If my uncle hated me this much, and the witches hate shifters enough to systematically annihilate their kind... what other kinds of hate exist in the world?

Is there anything good at all?

Is anything worth saving?

Warm hands gently press against mine, and I fall out of the panic-induced flashbacks. Suddenly, I'm back in the cabin, only I'm on the floor now. I must have slipped from the chair during my attack.

Archer kneels in front of me, concern touching his green eyes and his face smooth with kindness. "Sable? Can you hear me?"

I nod, but I keep nodding. Nodding like a crazy person. I can't stop the damn nodding, like the bones holding my head in place have given up.

Archer's hands move from my fists to my face. His fingers are strong but gentle as he slows the frantic nodding. Reaching up, I cling to his wrists, my weight resting almost entirely against his hold on my head. He grounds me, an anchor in the storm.

Our eyes lock together as he says, "Breathe with me." He makes an exaggerated O with his lips, pulling in air loudly.

I mimic his movements, exaggerated and all. Keeping my eyes on his face, I follow his deep breaths in and out while the warmth in his hands soothes the ice flooding through my veins. It's only me and Archer, and there's no room left for the panic. A soothing calm rolls over me, grounding me.

I feel like I could fall into the depths of his eyes.

Like I could fall and keep falling.

And I don't know if that's a good thing or a bad thing.

18

SABLE

For the next several days, the four of us spend nearly every waking moment together, falling into a comfortable routine. After that first evening when Archer had to pull me out of my panic-fueled flashback, all three men treat me with gentle compassion—even Trystan, who I doubt such empathy comes easy to.

And thanks to their awareness, I don't have another panic attack.

Plus, exactly as Ridge promised me, they leave me alone at night to sleep in the one bed by myself, while they curl up in wolf form on the living room floor. I'm so thankful for their attentiveness to my feelings, but I can't help the guilt that twinges my chest. The floor isn't nearly as comfortable and warm as the bed, and to be honest, when we say good night, I feel an emptiness that carries me through the night and isn't filled until I wake up to the sounds and smells of them making breakfast every morning.

Something inside me feels like it's trapped. Locked away and desperate to reach out and touch these three men.

My body just won't obey.

It's like I'm broken—like maybe that part of me will never work again. Never had a chance to work in the first place, even. My uncle beat the capacity to love someone, to truly connect with someone, right out of me.

Maybe that was his plan from the start.

On our fourth day in the cabin, I lounge on the front steps, watching as my three companions split firewood in the yard. They're passing an axe around between them, and they've stripped off their shirts. Despite the brisk chill in the air, their torsos are shiny with exertion as they take turns chopping logs on a sawed-off tree stump.

I'm having a hard time not staring, and an even harder time not drooling. It's clear they're showing off for me.

The cabin is fairly rustic—we're cooking our meals over the fire in the fireplace, and much of our dinners have come from the men shifting and hunting. The running water for the shower comes from a rain basin, while the electricity comes from a generator that's typically off all day and only used for a small portion of the evening. Regardless, there's already a giant pile of cut firewood against the side of the cabin, yet here we are.

Trystan shoves Ridge out of the way with his elbow and raises the axe, casting a glance my way as if to make sure I'm watching before he brings it down on the log. Then Ridge steps around Trystan, giving me another telling look before he sets up a log and does the same.

Biting my lip to hide an amused smile, I dig my toe into the dirt by the front steps.

Truthfully, I can't help but *like* the way they're showing off for me.

The attention is a balm to my broken heart, and it balances out all the years I lay alone in my bed in my uncle's house, wondering if I'd ever have a friend or a reason to even live.

But beyond the friendly competition, I can sense real tension between the men—all of them, even Archer, the sweetest and most level-headed of the three.

I hate that tension. Things they've said, jabs they've taken at each other, all of it adds up to my impression that despite their treaty, their three packs are at odds with each other and have been for some time. Adding me to the mix as a potential mate for all three of them has only fueled the already smoldering fire.

"Sable," Archer calls, jarring me from my thoughts.

"Hm?" I look at him, standing in a patch of sunlight that spills through the trees. His tanned skin shines like it's illuminated from within, and the way he's resting the axe handle on his shoulder displays the muscles in his chest.

"You're up. Come give it a try," he says, holding up another—smaller—axe with a smile. "You might feel better if you take some of your anger out on firewood."

I can't exactly argue that point. I broke a few things in my time living with Clint when everything got to be too much, although I usually paid for it later or took great pains to clean up and hide the mess.

Still...

"I don't know," I say, eyeing the weapon. "It looks hard. And dangerous."

Ridge stretches out his shoulders, grinning at me as he jerks his chin in invitation. "We'll teach you."

His voice warms my insides and chases away the lingering misgivings I have. I hop to my feet and join them in the patchy sunlight, taking the offered axe from Archer. It's lighter than I expected but still has heft to it. A few swings will probably work out muscles I didn't even know I had.

Ridge steps up behind me, reaching around to place my hands in position. "You'll have better control if you keep your hands separate," he advises, his breath tickling my ear. A tingle starts low in my body, and I have to fight the urge to sink back against his bare chest, to nuzzle into his skin and breathe deeply of his familiar pine scent.

Archer places a round log atop the stump and then backs away, well out of range of the crazy girl with the axe.

Smart man.

"Ready?" Ridge asks, and I nod. "Place the axe on the log as a starting point. It'll help with muscle memory."

I do what he says, resting the blade in the center of the log. He disappears from my back, and when I'm sure he's at a safe distance, I heave the axe up and let it fly.

I miss the log completely, metal sinking into the tree stump.

"Good form." Archer steps in and yanks the axe from the wood, whirling it around to hand it to me, handle first. "The first try is *always* a swing and a miss. Let's do it again."

They take turns showing me their methods, giving me advice while giving each other shit. After a few more misses, I finally hit the log, and a few more swings after that, I've really got the hang of it.

But cutting the firewood isn't the true stress reliever, I realize. Yeah, sure, it's *really* nice to imagine the log is my uncle's face. And I do that a few times.

As tension evaporates from my body and the knot in my stomach starts to unwind, I finally realize what it really is.

It's these men.

Their attention. Their friendly, easy-going banter. The way they look out for me and take care of me.

I've never had anything like that in my life, and try as I might to resist, I feel myself being drawn toward them like a flower toward sunlight.

THAT NIGHT, I slip into an easy sleep, though my arm muscles do their best to protest.

At first my dreams are benign and nonsensical.

I'm racing through the forest with the cold mountain wind ruffling my hair. I see wolves around me and the moon high overhead, and my body feels lighter than air, as if I'm flying rather than running. I reach the edge of a ravine, and rocks shift and fall beneath my feet.

Then Ridge is beside me in human form—naked and magnificent, even in my dreams. He takes my hand and we jump right over the edge of the canyon. Instead of falling, we soar.

But then it isn't Ridge beside me anymore.

His hand becomes a vise grip, and I'm lying on my uncle's work bench with my hand in an actual vise grip. Both hands are pinned between unforgiving metal planks on either side of my body. I can't struggle. It only makes the pain worse to try.

Uncle Clint towers over me, smoke curling up over his balding head from the cigarette perched between his lips. He lifts a hand, and I see he's holding a cutting knife—a small one from our kitchen set, meant for chopping vegetables, not for slicing up your niece.

But that's what he uses it for.

This is one of his calculated torture sessions, I realize in horror. Not his drunken rages or his power-hungry man tantrums that cause him to push me down stairs or punch me in soft places on my body.

This is war.

This is tactical.

His knife slices up the front of my shirt, and he uses the sharp tip to throw the edges of my shirt out of his way. He eyes my stomach like a painter planning his next move, before he sets the blade to my skin and starts to carve.

Even in my dream, the ghost of the pain feels almost as horrible as it did in real life. He carves so lightly, not deep enough that it won't properly heal. In his calculated attacks, my uncle scratches some kind of itch I've never understood. He wants me to feel maximum pain. He wants to cause me excruciating agony. And he knows how to cover his tracks well enough to get away with it.

Blood runs down my sides in warm little rivulets, soaking through the crumpled fabric of my destroyed t-shirt. The cuts keep going until I'm screaming, screaming for anybody to help me. Screaming for something to take me away from this pain.

I wake up in a cold sweat, my heart pounding like a jackhammer against my ribcage. The blankets are heavy on my body, more confining than they should be, and I frantically shove them off me with all four limbs until they slip off the bed to pool on the floor.

My breaths come faster as I glance around the dark

room. I can hear that the generator is off beyond the cabin wall, so I can't even turn on a light to dispel the gloom.

The small bedroom feels like a tomb, and all logic flees in the face of my panic.

I'm trapped.

I can't be here anymore.

So I slip out of bed and rush out of the back door of the cabin, where the moon shines brightly on the forest and I don't have to be in the dark with my nightmares.

19
DARE

Iт's the kind of night made for stealth.

The kind of night made for tracking down witches and destroying each and every one of them before they can find a way to penetrate pack lands.

The landscape flashes by at warp speed, and my paws thunder against the ground. I live for this shit—this freedom, the wild air, the heady scent of dirt.

The chase.

I skid to a stop in a small clearing just beyond the barrier line and lift my nose to the air. I can smell her—the witch that's been testing the boundaries of our sigils. She has a cold scent, calculating and authoritarian, like she's an alpha in her own right.

The good news is, alphas are born to be tested.

And beaten.

I duck between the trees and put my nose to the

ground just beyond the barrier. A tentative scent pattern tells me the witch was here, and recently. She zig-zagged just outside the boundary, getting closer and closer with every fucking step. I've been tracking this bitch for weeks, and as always, it seems I'm still one step behind her.

No matter. She can't evade me forever.

As I pass back through the boundary, I catch a hint of something different. Not the witch's scent, but something sweeter and more alluring.

I follow the marker to a nearby tree and jump up onto my hind legs to sniff at the tree. A female. Not any pack member that I know, but still somehow familiar.

I consider following it, but I haven't finished my patrols. The East, West, and North Packs aren't handling the witch threat as aggressively as they should, which leaves me to pick up the slack and do their dirty work.

Without a pack of my own to protect, I figure what else is there to do but protect the rest of the packs from their own inadequacies?

Heading west, I follow the narrow corridor of empty land between the West and North Packs, focusing for the witch's scent. I run for several miles before I'm satisfied by the fact she hasn't yet come this way. The boundaries are still strong, humming with power and untouched by her magic.

That's good—it means she's sticking to the farthest boundaries, closest to the more populated human lands.

Whether that's because she hasn't found the empty lands between the pack territories, or because she hasn't tried, I don't know.

I'm not going to give her a chance to try.

Every night, I complete my patrol. I start on the farthest western boundaries and make the circuit all the way around, then through the empty lands between each of the three packs' territories. Without fail, I spend my nights protecting the dumbasses who can't protect themselves.

What the fuck are they even doing all day?

I slow my pace and veer off the path to take a break and get some water, letting that thought mull in my head and stoke the anger that seems to have taken up permanent residence in my chest.

They could be planning and prepping to add more protections, to do *more* for the shifters. Instead, I caught wind recently that they'd had more executions. More wolves dead. They let the witches get close enough to kill their people.

Fucking idiots.

I sink to my haunches on the bank of my usual stream and drink. This deep in the mountains, the water tastes wild and untamed, so crisp it sends shivers through me.

Then I scent something that doesn't belong here.

Raising my nose to the breeze, I sniff the wind. It's that same stranger's smell—the female, something not quite shifter, but familiar. I stand and turn into the oncoming wind, realizing it's bringing that intoxicating smell from farther upstream.

I can't help myself. I follow it.

A half-moon shines down through the trees as I take my time walking the banks of the stream. It's the darkest depths of night, when the sky is full of stars and the moon transforms the land into something unearthly. I feel most myself during these hours, as if my wolf is so fully connected to the land that I've lost track of the human inside me.

I'm a decent distance from any of the three packs' settlements. I never see anyone out this way except wildlife.

So I'm shocked as hell to come across a woman.

She's sitting on the edge of the stream with her feet in the water, watching with the hint of a smile on her face as the current races over her skin. The moonlight turns her hair almost white and her pale skin nearly translucent, as if she's glowing from the inside.

She's the most beautiful thing I've ever seen.

Another light breeze races past me, and that strange scent hits my nose again.

Mine.

The thought comes from nowhere and everywhere, and a force inside me rises up so strongly I stagger on my paws. This woman is mine, I realize, instantly shifting back to human form. There's nothing in the world right now that could stop me from having her.

My feet are silent on the grass as I stride toward her, drawn as if by a magnetic pull. I'm surrounded by that intoxicating scent, and my wolf snarls inside me, urging me to move faster. So I do.

I'm so aware of her every movement that I notice the exact second she senses my approach. Her head pops up, and she looks down the bank at me, blue eyes luminous and wide. Her fear rises on the air, adding to her natural scent, and I growl under my breath. I don't like that she's afraid. She has no reason to be.

I would kill for her and die for her, but I would never fucking hurt her.

Before she can react, I'm standing over her. I grip her by both arms and haul her to her feet until we're chest to chest. God, this close, she smells like every delicious thing I've ever wanted and didn't know I could have.

I dip my head and brush my nose along her neck, breathing in her scent like a drug.

I've found her.

The woman I never knew I've always been looking for.

My mate.

20

SABLE

THIS CAN'T BE REAL.

It's the only thought my stunned mind can form as a torrent of emotions rage through me.

My heart crashes against my ribs as the man's fingers dig into my arms, holding me tight against his body. His *naked* body, flush to mine from thigh to chest. There's something hot and hard pressed against my belly that sends waves of fire through me—because I know what it is, and it's as alluring as it is terrifying.

I don't know how this happened. I just wanted some fresh air.

The water felt so good on my feet, and the moonlight made the forest and everything around me glow with the light I needed so badly after my nightmares.

But then I wasn't alone anymore. Suddenly, this man

came out of nowhere, pulling me up and hauling me against his body.

Jesus, it's glorious. He's glorious.

I'm swelling with a mixture of shock and fear at his bruising grip and the way he dragged me to my feet. He's aggressive, much more so in his movements than Ridge, Trystan, or Archer, and I know this entire situation should terrify me beyond anything I've experienced so far. I'm alone, in the middle of the night, with a strange, aroused man touching my body.

But the heavy dose of my own desire is keeping me from dipping over the edge into panic. He calls to something wild in me. This isn't like when my uncle used to manhandle me or hurt me. This is something altogether different, and the warmth between my legs responds with a delicious ache.

His nose brushes the sensitive skin just above my collarbone, and he breathes deeply, sliding his face up my neck and into my hair. I know innately that he's a shifter, because no normal human man would breathe my skin like that, as if he's learning all the secrets of my soul in just one sniff.

He pulls away, just enough for our gazes to meet. My hands are bunched up between us, but still free. I think, if I could get my traitorous body to listen, I could break out of his grip. If I wanted to.

But I don't want to.

God fucking help me, I don't.

For a long moment, we just stare at each other, taking each other in. He's devastatingly handsome. Big and strong, with spiky black hair that's windswept and messy, brown eyes flecked with gold, and a strong jaw on a sharp-angled face.

I... I *recognize* him.

"It's you," I whisper, my eyes flaring wide. The man who nearly hit me the night I ran away from my uncle. I recall vividly the way his car skidded sideways before my hands slapped the metal, our eyes locking in mutual shock.

Now his eyes widen too, and his gaze sweeps over my face again as if he's trying to put the pieces together himself. One hand releases my arm and his fingers slide up to brush against my face.

He cocks his head, the movement so animalistic he might as well still be in wolf form.

"You hit my car." His voice is a deep rumble.

"Sorry about that," I murmur, even though if anybody should be sorry, it's *him*. He could have killed me. But I'm too distracted by the tingles his fingers are sending along my nerve endings. Some part of me recognizes that he's released me. He's not holding me against him anymore.

I could back away. I could run. I could scream for Ridge and the others.

Then the man's fingers slip into my hair. A fresh jolt of electric sensation skitters through me as he fists the strands lightly, holding them close to the roots. It's not painful, but there's something so commanding, so dominant in the gesture, that it makes a flush of liquid heat fill my core.

"What's your name?"

"Sable." The whisper comes out hoarse, and even I can hear the desire underlying it. I want this man. Something within me wants this man, and she's roaring to have him. I struggle to clamp down on that crazy sensation, on the overwhelming need to crawl into his arms. "You?"

"Dare."

A thrill tickles along my spine. Even though I know he's telling me his name, it almost sounds like a command on its own.

Dare you.

I've never considered myself brave or reckless or daring. I've lived a great deal of my life in fear, tiptoeing around my uncle and measuring days in degrees of awfulness. Before running away from Clint, I rarely thought about what I *did* want, focusing instead on what I didn't.

But right now, as I stare up into this beautiful stranger's eyes, all I can think about is the one thing I want most in the entire world. The thing that calls to me like the moon calls to a wolf, begging me to reach out and take it.

Dare you.

Before I know what's happening, before I can register whether he moved first or I did, I'm on my tiptoes, my body pressed against his.

And I'm kissing him.

His grip on my hair tightens a little, angling my head as he kisses me back, and the small bite of pain sends another shock of arousal through me. His other hand wraps around me, his palm cupping my ass to tug me tighter against his erection. As I wrap my arms around his neck, he opens his mouth, his tongue licking along my lips. The motion sends heat spiraling through me, and I move against him, the hard length of him sliding between us.

Our kiss deepens, tongues dancing. My nightgown bunches beneath his hand, and his fingers dip deeper, brushing the outer boundaries of territory that no man has ever touched. I don't even know him, but that doesn't make a single difference to me in this moment as I open my legs wider, practically begging for him to keep searching, to go farther.

The kiss deepens until I'm drowning in him, in his taste, in the wild scent of him. His hand moves from my hair to my chest, and he palms my breast, his thumb brushing over the peak of my nipple in a slow movement that sets my body on fire. I arch into his hand, my fingers tangling in his hair.

I want more.

So much more.

I feel like I'm outside myself as I lift a leg and wrap it around his hips. Nothing separates us now but the thin cotton of my underwear, and it's still too damn much. I rub against him, reveling in his gasp against my lips. He grabs my thigh, hauling my leg higher, opening me wider. My body has a mind of its own, and the feeling of his hard length rubbing against my core outside my panties turns me even more mindless with need.

"Jesus. You taste like fucking sunshine," he growls, dragging his mouth from mine before moving his lips downward to press against the curve of my jaw.

A shiver runs down my spine, and I hold on to him for dear life as he devours the skin of my throat, scraping his teeth over the sensitive flesh. I didn't know it could feel like this, to have a man's lips on that part of my body. I'm growing a little more familiar with the way a kiss can spread heat all the way through my limbs, warming me up from the inside out.

But this?

I can hardly catch my breath as he nips and sucks at my skin, sending bursts of sensation skittering through me. When he draws my earlobe into his mouth and bites down on it, I let out a soft cry, digging my fingernails into his shoulders as I grind against him.

How is this possible? How can one body contain all the feelings tearing through me right now?

"Dare!"

I gasp the word, whimpering this stranger's name as if I've known him my whole life. As if I've called out his name like this hundreds of times before.

He pulls back from me a little, wrapping one arm around my lower back while the other catches my chin, tilting my face up toward his. My fingers have been in his hair, making the dark spiky locks even wilder than they were before, and his eyes look almost black in the shadowy light.

"Say it again," he murmurs. "Say my name."

He's not even kissing me anymore, but the low rumble of his voice sends a tremor of pleasure through me. My breath catches, and I bite my bottom lip as my chest rises and falls fast.

"Dare."

"Sable."

Wolves don't purr. I know they don't. But that's the only way to describe the way he says my name.

My core clenches, goose bumps breaking out on my skin. His lower half is still pressed right up against me, his arm around my back keeping our bodies pinned together. My panties are slick, the fabric absorbing the wetness that's seeping from me, and I wonder dazedly if he can tell. Can he feel it? Can he feel it against his naked skin?

As if he can read my thoughts, Dare's nostrils flare. He drags in a deep breath, then drops his head again, his fingers gripping my jaw tighter as he brings his lips to mine once more.

Before the kiss can go any deeper, three distinct growls erupt from the silence of the night around us.

21

SABLE

I BREAK away from Dare's lips, shock flooding me.

What... what just happened?

Ridge, Trystan, and Archer in their wolf forms race over the ground from the cabin. I can feel their energies from here—their protective, animal instincts are turned on full blast, and they're ready to rip Dare from limb to limb.

I know what it probably looks like. Me, alone by the stream in just my short nightgown, and a naked wolf shifter with his hands on my body and his lips on mine, while the other three men have done their damndest to get to know me, to ease me into a relationship without the benefit of persuading me with touch.

None of them have given in to their wolves. They've respected my boundaries and refused to let their beasts just *take* me like they own me.

Like Dare did.

Like I let him.

My three companions race toward us, snapping and growling in a show of aggression that sets my heart pumping and makes me want to flee into the woods. Panic rears up swiftly inside me, dousing my desire like a bucket of cold water on a flame.

Dare releases me, his own growl rumbling up from deep within his chest. He puts himself between me and the other men as if trying to protect me, and then the now-familiar mirage of magic shimmers over his body as he shifts to wolf form. Dare is massive, with midnight black fur that almost seems to camouflage into the night.

The four wolves come together in a violent clash of teeth and claws, their snarls breaking the peace of the night.

It's three against one. For the first time since this all began, Ridge, Trystan, and Archer are completely united against something they see as a common enemy—Dare. The horrifying realization that he doesn't have a chance against their ferocity sends my heart into palpitations.

Ridge's pale brown wolf gets hold of Dare's neck, and though he's smaller than the latter wolf, Ridge takes Dare down to the dirt. The black wolf hits the ground hard on his side, Ridge's teeth latched onto his neck, but manages to buck out of his grasp and roll away—back on his feet so fast, it's almost like it never happened.

Trystan and Archer leap in, jaws snapping at Dare's

legs. Ridge bares his teeth before leaping onto Dare's back again, and a pained yelp tears through the night.

Something snaps inside me.

This fight *isn't* fair.

Whatever force is connecting me to Ridge, Trystan, and Archer, it's identical to whatever connected me to Dare. He acted on that connection, and I allowed him.

I race forward, barely cognizant of the rough ground beneath my bare feet. I don't even think twice before I throw myself bodily between the wolves, putting Dare at my back. Trystan, who just lunged at the black wolf, has to redirect at the last minute so he doesn't hit me, and Archer immediately sits down on his haunches, his head cocked in surprise.

I hold my hands up between them all, my face hard and fear pumping through my veins.

Jumping into the middle of a wolf fight wasn't the smartest thing I'd ever done—in fact, it has to make the list of top five *stupidest* things I've ever done—but at least no one accidentally ripped me to shreds before they realized what was happening.

Archer is the first to shift back to human form, crouching on the ground naked just as he was as a wolf. His transformation sets off a domino effect, with Ridge turning back next, then Dare, and finally Trystan.

None of them look happy about the situation. They all

look furious—except maybe Archer, whose enigmatic expression remains neutral.

I keep my gaze firmly above everyone's shoulder-level as I lower my hands. My heart feels like it's on the verge of exploding inside me, and I suck in a deep breath, then another, trying to calm the damn thing so I can speak with more authority than I feel.

"I won't let you fight," I say. My voice sounds thin and weak at first, but it gains strength as I find my footing. "I don't know what this thing is between us. Or between me and Dare either," I add, motioning to the quiet, brooding man behind me. "But I refuse to let you hurt each other because of it."

22

ARCHER

HOLY FUCK. She's magnificent. Single-handedly the most beautiful thing I've ever seen, standing between us with her hair wild and a hard glint in her eye.

I can scent her fear. There's a tension in her body that speaks to a deep urge to run, the way a deer would bolt at the crack of a twig in the night. But she doesn't. She stands there, chin in the air, stance wide and unmoving, despite the four powerful, intimidating shifters staring her down.

Sable, my beautiful mate, refuses to bend, and this glimpse of the warrior inside her—the wolf inside her—sends a wave of warmth and respect through me.

Back in the council's meeting house, I felt an instant and undeniable connection to her because of the mate bond. Not exactly a bond a shifter can ignore, or have any control over at all, really. But every day we've spent together since, I've learned more about her, gotten to know what makes her tick. It's only made me care for her more.

She's an amazing woman. Stronger than she even knows. Soft but unbreakable, vulnerable but with a spine of steel. Now it's more evident than ever what a firecracker she really is. I don't know her whole back story, though I've pieced some clues together and built my own theory. But if her previous life is as bad as I suspect, I know how much strength it takes for her to stand up in the face of violence.

And she just threw herself in the middle of serious violence.

Her voice wobbles as she goes on. "Just stop this. Now. You're not monsters."

It's the crack on the last word that makes my protective hackles raise. She's losing that initial steam, and her past trauma is overtaking her resolve and anger. From my own experience, I know she's about to crumble.

So I go to her.

I hear a low growl from Trystan's direction, like that fucker has any business trying to calm a broken woman. I don't give a rat's ass if he's pissed I'm taking control. I don't care if any of them are pissed about it.

Sable barely moves as I gather her into my arms. She's stiff, her entire body shivering, not from the cool air but from her emotions. It takes her a few seconds to relax into my embrace and sink against me. Her arms finally wrap around my waist, and she presses her face into my chest just before tears crest over her cheeks.

I cup the back of her head, letting my fingers play over the satin strands of her hair. "Shh. It's okay. Breathe through it. Like we did before, you remember?"

She immediately follows my order, her chest rising and falling with deep, even breaths against my torso. The press of her breasts against me and the rest of her soft form flush against mine, separated only by the thin cloth of her nightgown, makes my body react immediately.

I can still smell her arousal, still sense hints of the way her body responded to Dare. I fight not to get hard, but it's almost impossible with her this close. Between the mix of her lingering scent and her curves against me, it's not an easy battle.

I don't want to scare her. I want to be there for her.

So I focus my gaze on Trystan's dumb ass as a means to deflate.

Nobody moves for several long moments. Sable's crying silently, her tears wet on my skin. The good news is she's not lost in her panic like she was the first night we arrived. So I keep petting her hair and tell her, "You're okay. Everything's going to be okay," over and over as the moon rides higher in the sky.

Eventually, even the tension from our companions dies away. The alpha anger fades from the air, and they stand down as concern for Sable replaces the fury. Gotta hand it to them—they adapt fast and put her first.

As mates should.

Is it really possible that we're all connected to her by a mate bond? It's a surreal concept. We're not the only shifter packs in the world, so I know there are more wolves out there who might have seen multiple mates that we wouldn't know of.

But in our circles, one wolf mates with one wolf. Period.

These men—even Dare, whose dark presence stands just to my left, bleeding concern for Sable—are alphas in their own right. They're born and bred to take whatever the hell they want, whenever they want it. And yet, they put her needs first.

It speaks volumes. Volumes I really don't fucking understand.

Her tears and sniffles have slowed. I pull back just enough to tilt her chin up with a finger so that our gazes meet. Moonlight washes over her face, turning her into a silver ray of light with big, sad eyes that touch me to my core.

"None of us want to hurt you," I murmur softly, sliding my other hand between us so that I can entwine our fingers. I lift her knuckles to my lips. "We'll figure this out. Without fighting."

Someone growls. Probably fucking Trystan again, though to be fair, Ridge isn't looking at Dare with any level of respect right now either.

I get it. We're all suspicious, all angry with each other for being in the way of what feels like the most natural thing in the world to us—our bond with Sable.

Regardless, I know they're capable of putting her first, and I'm not going to let them forget it.

Sable's fingers open inside mine so that she can touch the side of my face. It's such a sweet gesture, and her wide-eyed gaze is completely innocent of the effect she has on me, but she's so damn beautiful it makes me wish I was more feral like Dare. More willing to close the space between us and take her lips as if they belong to me.

Because I'm *certain* they do.

I let my gaze drop to that perfect, red cupid's bow of her mouth, and I imagine what she would taste like. Bad idea though, as desire shoots straight down between my legs before I can look at Trystan and wash away the heated thoughts with how much he irritates me.

Sable's breath hitches, and she releases my hand before pushing away from me. She's just realized she's hugging a naked man, because the naked man couldn't keep it down in her presence.

Goddammit.

I do my fucking best to be the bigger man, to be the

better man, and in the end, I'm ruled by my dick no more or less than any of these other shifters.

I glance at Dare. "Come on, man. You better come inside. We should get dressed."

23

SABLE

THE FIVE OF us troop into the cabin, Ridge at the head of our little group. I hang back in the living room while the men go to the bedroom to dig clothes out of the packs. Thank God for that—I'm on naked man overload.

My fingers are still shaking as I locate a box of wood matches and light the few candles scattered around the living room. Ridge will probably protest and say we can afford to turn on the generator for this, but I don't want the harsh overhead light right now. I want to hide in the flickering shadows and come down from whatever the hell that was.

I'm on edge, my mind whirling and trying to come to grips with what just happened. The sudden emotional crashes back to back, from desire to fear to anger to despair, left me an emotional pile of hormones. I want to go crawl back into bed and pretend none of this ever happened.

But the way Dare kissed me...

Jesus, it was like nothing I've ever experienced before. The whole thing should have terrified me, sent me running for the cabin or screaming for help. I should have hated it, hated his hands on me, hated the way he dominated me.

Instead, I'm still craving him. Craving more of him, while simultaneously wondering what Ridge's skin would feel like under my fingers. How Trystan's mouth would taste, hot and wet on my lips. How agonizingly torturous Archer's hands would be on the most secret parts of my body...

Dare has cracked open something inside me, some kind of deep need I can't quite come to terms with.

The men all return together, trooping from the bedroom with comically identical looks on their faces. Ridge and Archer have covered up completely with shirts and sweats, but Trystan and Dare have left their chests bare and I'm pretty certain they're having some kind of manly, *my muscles are prettier than yours* face off.

I can't even pretend to understand men. Especially not when I've lost all comprehension of myself.

My three companions take positions around me on the couch and matching armchair, while Dare stands near the door as if preparing to run, should the need arise. Considering the way Ridge, Trystan, and Archer banded together to destroy him in the yard, I can hardly blame him. He's the new guy, the new *competition*, and as far as they're concerned he doesn't belong.

I know otherwise.

When I lock gazes with Dare, he's looking at me with intense, hungry eyes, broadcasting how much he wishes we could have finished what we started. He certainly doesn't seem regretful or sorry about what happened.

Honestly, I can't say that I am either.

Looking away from his dark eyes, I take a couple more breaths. If I have to breathe any deeper or harder to ground myself, I'm going to pass out.

Ridge leans on the arm of the couch and levels his calculating gaze on Dare. "What were you doing out this way?"

"Patrolling," Dare says shortly. Inside the cabin, his voice booms, even deeper than I realized outside. "Hunting for a witch who's been sniffing around the boundaries." His gaze cut to me. "I was nearby when I caught Sable's scent. I followed it to her, and my wolf felt the mate bond."

Trystan groans, laying his head back on the edge of the couch, but Ridge says, "It's not your job to patrol the boundaries."

"No, it's not," Archer adds, his brow wrinkled with annoyance. "What happens when you get yourself killed?"

Fury rises on Dare's face, and he crosses his arms, glaring at each man in turn. "If the packs were doing a better job of fighting the witch threat, I wouldn't feel the need to patrol."

"We're doing all we can," Ridge argues.

"Then why are your wolves dying?"

Four voices rise in anger as they start arguing and talking over one another.

"You're all completely unaware of how bad things are!" Dare roars, pointing at them. "Your sheltered fucking pack life, completely out of touch with how bad things are getting—"

"Hey, fuck you," Trystan snaps, leaping up from the couch with his hands balled into fists.

The yelling gets louder.

A few weeks ago, Trystan's looming show of brute force would have sent me spiraling into a panic attack. And for a moment, his giant hands curled into weapons do raise a hint of terror in me. But I do what Archer always tells me —deep breaths, in and out, until the sight of Trystan's fists don't alarm me anymore.

I don't get why they're all so worked up over this. Clearly, the witches are a threat, and they all already work together for the good of the entire local shifter nation. Why is it such a bad thing that Dare was patrolling?

There's too much energy in this room. Too much "alpha" and not enough logical thought.

"Hey!" I blurt, my voice almost falling flat under the

rise in volume. I raise my tone that much more and shout, "Knock it off!"

The cabin goes silent. All four men look at me as if they're surprised to learn my voice can get that loud.

"What on earth is going on?" I say, looking around at them all and trying not to blush under their combined gazes. "You're all on the same team here. Why are you ganging up on Dare?"

Trystan, still looming over the couch with dislike twisting his facial expression, sighs. "Dare was the alpha of the South Pack—before it was splintered and destroyed by witches."

"What?" My voice drops to a whisper.

"It happened a few years ago. They must've planned it for months. It wiped out most of the pack and sent the survivors fleeing into the mountains." Ridge speaks evenly, but his controlled tone only serves to highlight the awfulness of his words.

I blink several times, absorbing this new—and alarming—information.

Dare's *entire* pack was destroyed by witches?

I look at the black-haired man for confirmation, hoping he'll tell me that Trystan's just being an asshole. That Ridge is just exaggerating or making things sound worse than they really are. But for the first time in the short time Dare has been around me, he doesn't have that wild, cocky confidence in his expression.

He looks haunted.

Pained.

It's true. Witches eliminated his entire pack, leaving him all alone.

I cover my mouth, tears pricking my eyes. That horrible expression on his face makes my heart ache. I want to go to him, to fix him, to heal him somehow from that level of hurt. He's all alone in the world, and clearly carrying an insane amount of guilt and heartache.

Before I can make a decision to get up and cross to him, he turns away from us all. I watch, heartbroken, as he shakes his head and appears to be gathering himself from the depths of his emotions.

"The reason I patrol," he says, voice soft and dangerous as he speaks over his shoulder, "is because what happened to my pack could happen again. It is my *privilege* to hunt the witches and protect my race."

My heart twists at the raw tone of his voice. I know I'm in the dark on a lot of things regarding the history of the packs and the witch threat, but Dare's situation brings the horrifying truth to light. An entire pack destroyed...

How is that even possible?

And are the other packs in danger of the same thing?

Ridge and Archer exchange glances that are weighed down with concern. Even Trystan, who clearly doesn't like Dare, looks like he wishes he hadn't said anything. They're either concerned about Dare being out there on his own hunting the witches, or they're concerned he's carrying the weight of it all too heavily. Maybe both.

I have those same thoughts. Dare, come what may, is still my possible mate, and the five of us are now like a strange little family. I can't stand aside and let him go back out there. What if he truly *is* my mate? And I just let him go get killed without giving our bond a proper chance?

"You can stay with us," I say, before anyone has a chance to speak.

Trystan growls. "I hardly think that's—"

"Dare can stay here." My voice gains a little strength, and I square my shoulders. "He's no different than any of you. His wolf sees me as his mate too."

Trystan's face is thunderous, and he remains looming over the couch, fists clenched, though he doesn't make a move anywhere. Ridge casts a wary look at Dare, but then sinks back against the couch cushions with a sigh.

Archer seems to be the only man who's truly accepting of this turn of events. I'm glad to have at least one logical shifter on my side.

Dare meets my gaze, and I can tell he's torn. As he told us, he feels a duty to hunt the witches, and I totally get that. Especially since he said he was in the middle of tracking one when he caught scent of me. But the longer our gazes hold, the more heated and intense his expression grows.

He's remembering what happened on the bank of the stream. Just like I am.

"All right," he says stiffly. "I'll stay."

A flood of relief makes my stomach flutter, the reaction stronger than I expected. I didn't realize how nervous I was that Dare might not stay until he agreed not to leave.

Now he's staring at me with a look so intense it feels like my clothes might actually catch fire, and an overwhelming heat flushes through me. This night has been too much. Too many intense emotions, new revelations, and unanswered questions crammed into just a few hours have left me reeling.

Casting a look around the room, I stand up and stretch. "Um... it's late. We should all get some sleep. Do you think you guys can handle sharing a room?"

"We'll be fine," Ridge assures me. I believe him—he'll do what's best for all of us, even if he hates every minute along the way.

The bedroom is cool and dark as I slip beneath the covers again. I wasn't lying when I said I needed sleep, but as I lie awake staring up at the dark ceiling, I don't feel tired at all. Too many thoughts are whirling around in my mind.

What would have happened if I hadn't left the cabin tonight? If I hadn't had the nightmare that forced me to get some fresh air? We never would have known Dare was close by—and I never would have known I had yet another shifter vying for my bond.

God, that's so confusing.

Instead of three possible mates, I now have to choose between four. Even worse, the feeling inside me that I think might be my own wolf slowly waking from her slumber doesn't favor any of them over the other. She sees them *all* as hers.

I don't understand how I'm supposed to do this. It's going to be an impossible choice.

The men must not be tired either, because I can hear them speaking in low, soft voices in the living room. I recognize who's speaking by pitch, happy to hear that even Dare and Trystan are making an effort to be civil. I can't make out the words, but the rumble is comforting.

After a while, I fall asleep to the sound and drift into better dreams.

When I wake up to late morning sunlight, all four men are already up. I can hear the low murmur of their voices conversing from the back of the cabin. I slide out of bed and fish out one of Amora's loaned T-shirts and a pair of shorts from my pack, get dressed, then run my fingers through my hair before padding out to join them in the kitchen.

Archer is standing over the wood stove as something delicious sizzles in the cast-iron skillet. He looks up as I enter and offers me a brilliant smile. "Good morning. Sleep well?"

"After the late night interlude, yeah," I reply, passing him to join the others at the table.

There are already dishes waiting—a plate piled high with pancakes, a pitcher of warmed syrup, a dish of sausage patties, and a smaller bowl of scrambled eggs.

"We're having a feast," I observe as I sit between Dare and Trystan. I try to keep my tone teasing and flippant, but I'm dying to eat every last thing on this table. Breakfast at my uncle's usually ended at cereal or oatmeal—a full-course meal like this is something I'd only ever seen on television.

Archer dumps a few more sausage patties into the bowl. "I felt like we all deserved a nice breakfast."

After he takes his seat, we all fill our plates and set to work. For a while, I'm too involved in eating—and in enjoying every single bite—to pay attention to the conversation around me. Despite the tension that filled the room last night, the men seem to have settled into a more comfortable arrangement in the light of morning.

I have a mouth full of syrupy, sweet pancakes when there's a lull in the conversation, and Dare looks right at me and says, "What happened to you the night I almost hit you with my car?"

The kitchen falls silent. As one, the other three men turn to look at me, their gazes just as questioning as Dare's.

Ridge speaks up first, cocking his head to one side. "You two have met before?"

I finish chewing my bite of pancakes and wash it down with a slurp of coffee, buying me some time. I've refrained from telling the shifters much about my past beyond what they've already deduced—it's impossible to hide the scars on my skin, and I know Ridge got an eyeful of them when he changed my clothes.

I definitely haven't brought up the night I fled from Uncle Clint's truck though. It isn't even because I want to keep it from them, exactly. Talking about it just feels... hard.

But I don't get a sense of pity from Dare when he asks me. In his position, I'd probably want to know why a frightened, wild-eyed woman nearly made me drive off the road in the dark too.

"You were running," Dare adds, glancing around at the other shifters.

At that, Archer says quickly, "We don't ask about Sable's past."

Trystan shoots Dare a murderous look, and Ridge's shoulders tense as he grips his fork tightly, like he's considering whether he'll need to use it as a weapon or not.

Their protectiveness is sweet, truly. But I can't keep the pain of my past a secret any longer. I remember vividly

Dare's haunted eyes last night. He knows pain, just like Archer does. Just like they *all* probably do, to some degree. None of these men will judge me for the things I've survived. But maybe knowing those things will help them understand me better.

Help us connect more.

And no matter how unsure I was about all of this in the beginning, I'm coming to realize that I truly do want that.

I want to know these men, in every way possible.

"I *was* running," I admit, putting down my fork. Even if I've worked up the bravery to sit here and tell them my story, I've completely lost my appetite. "My parents both died a long time ago. I hardly remember them. I was raised by my uncle, who beat and abused me. Most of you have seen the scars."

The fury on Ridge's face is frightening in its intensity, while Archer is looking at me like he wants to take me in his arms and kiss each and every one of my wounds. Both Trystan and Dare are watching me intently, waiting to hear more with expressionless faces.

I clear my throat around the lump rising in it. "He kept me locked away most of my life. I really only got to leave the house when he hurt me enough to require medical care. Couldn't even play outside as a kid. I barely even knew where we lived beyond that it's a big white farmhouse on the outskirts of Big Creek."

It's talking about the isolation that finally makes me cry.

Crazy that I can easily tell four strangers how my uncle abused me with a completely straight face, but remembering all those days locked in my room, all those years without a comforting touch...

That's what breaks me.

Tears burn the backs of my eyes, stinging painfully with the effort it takes to hold them back.

"I never felt safe enough to run away," I say, self-conscious about the way the words come out weak and strangled. "If I tried and he caught me, I knew he would kill me. I never felt like it would be... I didn't even try. I was weak."

All four men are tense now, staring at me with a mixture of sympathy and rage. The rage, I know, isn't directed at me. But the sympathy washes over me like a cool breeze on a hot day, calming the rapid pounding of my heart a little.

"We were coming home from the hospital that night," I say, finally getting around to Dare's question as I meet his gaze. "He... pushed me down the stairs and thought he had broken my arm. The doctor tried to help me; he was suspicious of Clint and wanted to ask me questions alone. But I was too scared, even then. I threw away the lifeline he offered me."

My throat tightens as I swallow, remembering the pity in Doctor Patil's eyes.

"Then on the way back, a deer ran out in front of my uncle's truck. He slammed on the brakes and we came to a stop just in time. We were angled half across the road. I looked out and saw the deer we almost hit and realized *it* was freer than I was. I had this moment of absolute clarity, and I just—I just threw the door open and ran. Right in front of your car," I add with a shaky smile.

Silence falls over the room as I finish speaking.

I hate that I've brought down the mood. It was a nice breakfast, somewhat lighthearted and full of energy. A vast improvement over last night. And I've ruined that. Although my life story couldn't do anything *but* bring the mood down, even if it isn't my fault.

"I should have run sooner," I murmur, wrapping my fingers around the warm coffee mug in front of me. I finally lose my battle against the burning tears, and they spill over the corners of my eyes. "I should have been stronger."

To my left, Trystan shifts forward. He reaches out with one finger and brushes away the tear sliding toward my jaw line. My breath catches in my throat, my body reacting to his touch as if an electric current flows between us.

I look at him, our eyes meeting. He's such a proud, cocksure kind of guy, so hard to read, but his face is an open book right now.

Then, before I can fully process what he's doing, he leans in and kisses me.

It isn't hard or demanding, not like I would have expected from him. His lips lock with mine, warm and firm, sending a tingle up my spine, but he releases me without taking it further.

"You're not weak," he says gruffly, tucking his fingers into my hair and cupping my face gently. "You did whatever it took to survive. That's strength, Sable. The greatest kind of strength there is."

24

SABLE

TRYSTAN'S EYES are the most beautiful blue-green. They look like I imagine the ocean would look, and I feel like I'm drowning in them as he draws back a little, still holding my gaze.

He's such a confusing mix of conflicting pieces, this man. More of a mystery to me than any of the other three— even Dare, who I just met. Trystan often seems to look down at the rest of the world from on high, as if he's got everything figured out and is just waiting for everyone else to catch up.

But then he does things like this, and it's like a whole other side of him emerges.

A softer side.

A kinder side.

I want to know this side of him better. I want to understand him, to get inside his head.

His hand is still cupping my cheek, and we're gazing into each other's eyes as if we're the only two people in the world. But then Dare shifts slightly on one side of me, and Trystan's body gives a little jerk as he seems to remember we're not alone.

The veneer of casual, languid confidence falls back over his face, although softness still lingers in his eyes as he presses up to stand.

Ridge grips my hand gently. "He's right, Sable. I knew it as soon as I found you that night. You were all banged up, looking like a boxer who'd just gone eight rounds. Looking like a *fighter*."

I certainly didn't feel like a fighter that night. I was still nursing injuries from the man who abused me for most of my life as I fled through the woods like a frightened deer. What part of that does he suppose is representative of a fighter?

Maybe there are more ways to fight than just one, a quiet voice murmurs in my head. *Maybe sometimes running is fighting. Fighting to stay alive, just like Trystan said.*

"Thanks," I mutter quietly.

I'm fucking terrible at taking compliments, maybe because I haven't received many of them in my life. Clint was great at hurling insults, and I got pretty good at letting the harshest ones rebound off the armor I built around my heart.

But compliments?

My fortifications aren't meant to withstand those, and I don't quite know what to do with the warm feeling that floods my chest.

Archer leans in and presses a kiss to my cheek, his lips lingering for a second. When he pulls back, he gives me a little smile.

"I think today should be Sable Day," he says, glancing at the men gathered around me as he speaks. "It should be dedicated to doing something fun. Whatever Sable wants. What do you think?"

There are nods all around, and the warm feeling in my chest expands until it seems to fill my whole body. I'm positive I'm blushing a little as Archer looks back at me.

"Anything you'd like to do?"

"Um..." I chew on my lip, considering the question. "Could we go outside? I mean, farther away from the cabin than just to chop wood?"

I don't add that after spending so much of my life trapped in a single house, I'm developing a craving for open spaces and sunlight—but I don't need to. It seems like they can all sense my unspoken words anyway, and my suggestion is met with an enthusiastic response.

We clean up from breakfast, then head out the back door toward the stream where Dare found me last night. We turn right, following the edge of the small stream through the woods.

As the cabin disappears amidst the trees behind us, I slow my steps a little to fall in beside Ridge, who's bringing up the rear of the group.

"Is it safe for us to leave the cabin like this? I mean, I know you guys go out to hunt, but..."

"It's safe." He nods, although I don't miss the way his gaze stays alert as he takes in our surroundings. "As safe as it's possible to be with witches in the world anyway. We burned sigils into trees in a boundary that encompasses all of the pack lands. It's possible for witches to get through, but it makes it harder for them to come en masse. Harder for them to attack in numbers. And you're with four alphas." He glances down at me with a reassuring smile. "We won't let anyone hurt you."

I ignore the tingle that runs down my spine at the way he looks at me, focusing on what he just told me instead. "What do the sigils do? You've mentioned them before, but I don't really get it. Are they magic? I thought the only magic shifters had was... well, shifting."

"That *is* the only magic we have." Archer drops back to join us, ending up on my other side so I'm bookended by him and Ridge. "But sigils themselves hold power. Witches infuse them with magic, which makes them far stronger than any we could ever create. But anyone who knows how to form the proper sigils can wield the inherent power in those runes."

I blink, trying to process that new piece of information.

It's still sometimes hard to believe I'm having conversations where the word "magic" is said in total seriousness.

"So you use magic against the witches?"

"We use every tool we have against the witches," Ridge says, a hint of a growl entering his voice as he scans the trees again. Then he nudges me gently. "We use sigils for more than that though. Remember how your arm and ankle were nearly healed after your second night at my house? Our elders use sigils for a variety of purposes, including the creation of healing poultices and tinctures. And it's also how Elder Jihoon determined that there's wolf in you. His dowsing rods are powered by sigils."

It's hard to believe that was just over a week ago. It feels like it might as well be another lifetime, and the entirety of my upbringing in my uncle's house sometimes feels it must be just a very long, very horrible dream. Out here in the woods, with the sun shining and the birds twittering in the trees, it's hard to believe so much evil can exist in the world.

Of course, it *can*.

And I'll never be able to forget that.

I'll always bear the scars of my past, both the ones on the outside and the ones on the inside.

But right now, I can allow myself to believe that maybe —one day—they might fade.

We walk for several more minutes before the creek widens out into a small pond. Dare and Trystan got ahead of us, deep in a conversation that's the most civil I've seen them manage so far. By the time we catch up to them, Dare is kicking off his jeans. Trystan shoots me a wink before tugging his shirt over his head and shucking his jeans too.

Then magic ripples over both of them as they shift.

They pad toward the shoreline and step in, letting the water ripple around their paws. Beside me, Ridge gives one more scan of our surroundings before nodding to Archer. The two of them strip too, quickly and perfunctorily. Archer told me once that a shifter *could* make the transition fully clothed, but their clothes don't tend to survive the process. So to avoid wasting perfectly good clothing, they always undress first unless it's an emergency.

As I watch the two wolves join the others in the pond, a wave of unexpected longing washes through me.

I wish I could join them.

And I don't just mean in the water.

I wish I could shift too.

But I want Archer to get his wish. I want today to be a fun day, a lighthearted day, so I push any melancholy feelings aside and step forward, kicking off my shoes and rolling up my borrowed pants so I can wade in the shallows as the wolves splash around.

The water is probably runoff from higher up in the mountains, so it's just this side of freezing despite the warmth in the early spring air. It's crystal clear and has that crisp scent I love though, so I hold out as long as I can before my numb toes force me back onto land.

The men seem to take their cue from me, and as soon as I leave the water, they follow after me.

Dare gives a mighty shake, sending water spraying in all directions as his damp fur puffs out from his body. I laugh, holding up a hand to shield myself as the others all shake off too. When magic shimmers over their bodies, I suddenly take a great interest in the birds flitting among the branches above us—although I'd be lying if I said my gaze didn't slip back downward once or twice, catching on broad shoulders, thick thighs, and perfectly sculpted muscles.

After the men are all dressed again, we walk a little farther around the pond.

I find myself hiking next to Dare, and I can't stop myself from shooting little glances his way. I'm so curious about him, and I have dozens of questions I'm dying to ask. But even though I told the men my sad life story this morning, I'm hesitant to ask him about his.

I know the basics already—witches attacked his entire pack and sent the survivors scattering to the wind. Asking for more details feels a little like slowing down and gawking at the scene of an accident or something. I don't want to make him dredge up horrible memories just to satisfy my own morbid curiosity.

So when he catches me glancing at him for the third

time, I blurt out the first question I can think of that doesn't have to do with the decimation of his pack.

"Does it hurt?"

His brows furrow. "What?"

God, Sable. Be more awkward. Please.

I take a breath, then speak at a more normal speed. "The shift. When you turn from a man into a wolf or back. Does it hurt?"

His dark brown eyes focus on me, and I remember what they looked like last night in the moonlight, deep and mysterious. I wonder if I'll ever be able to look at him and not think of that moment. It feels like it's still imprinted on my skin, on my *soul*.

"Nah, it doesn't hurt." His gruff voice drags me from my thoughts. "Most of us start shifting when we're just cubs, so it might be a bit different for you. But it's not like being ripped apart and reformed. The magic washes through you and then it's done. It feels good in a way, like meeting your other half. Your better half."

His expression softens a little, and I wonder if he thinks his wolf is his better half. Do all shifters feel that way?

"That sounds... nice," I admit.

And it does. I was terrified by the idea that I might not be entirely human at first, but the idea isn't nearly as frightening as it once was.

What would I be like as a wolf? Would I be stronger

than I am as a human? More confident? Would I trust my instincts more?

Maybe Dare can see the wistfulness in my eyes, because he gives a soft snort. "I said *better*, not *perfect*. Wolves have good instincts, but we can make mistakes just like anyone."

For a second, I think maybe he's talking about the mate bond, and how four different shifters have somehow claimed that bond with me. But when I look up at him again, his features are hard, his gaze unfocused—and I realize he's thinking of something else entirely.

He's thinking of the thing I promised myself I wouldn't ask about.

"I'm sorry. About your pack."

The words come out before I can stop them. I press my lips together like that'll keep me from blurting out anything else as Dare's body goes stiff beside mine. We're walking close enough to each other that I can feel the change in him immediately, and my own body reacts to the tension in his.

"Thank you."

His voice is low and rough, and he doesn't meet my eyes as he speaks. I can't tell if I made anything better or just made everything worse. The overwhelming urge to reach out to him rises up in me, making my fingers itch to thread through his. I want to hold his hand or wrap my arms around his waist, and this impulse has nothing to do with the scorching heat that flared between us when he caged me in his embrace last night.

This urge is deeper and more complex than that.

I want to help him.

I want to heal him.

But I don't know if I can, or whether I even have a right to try. I don't know if he'd welcome that kind of touch from me, or what it would mean if he did.

So I just shoot him a soft smile and then move away to give him space, quickening my steps to join Archer and Trystan at the head of our little pack.

"Hey, Sable. You gettin' your sunshine fix?" Archer greets me with a grin, draping an arm over my shoulders.

"Yeah. Thanks."

I let myself melt against his body a little, my own arm instinctively going around his waist. It feels safe here. Comfortable.

When I glance over my shoulder, I find Dare watching me. The expression on his face is no longer hard and stoic. Instead, there's a softness in his features that makes me think maybe, just maybe, if I'd reached out—he would've let me.

25

SABLE

Over the next several days, things begin to shift between the five of us.

It's hard to believe how quickly these men have become a huge part of my life. I can barely remember when they *weren't* in my life, even though it was barely two weeks ago that Ridge found me in that ravine. There are still plenty of things I don't know about them and things they don't know about me. But I've stopped holding myself back as much, letting down little pieces of the barrier around my heart.

It meant more than I thought it would to tell my story out loud and have these four beautiful, protective men look at me the same way they did *before* they knew how fucked up my life has been.

I know they all hate my uncle, and I know they all hurt for me.

But they don't look at me like I'm broken.

Damaged.

Ruined.

They look at me like they always have, since pretty much the first moment I met them.

Like I'm special.

Like I'm perfect—just the way I am.

It's a balm to my soul, and their acceptance of even my broken parts makes it easier to trust them with more of myself. So I do.

We take more walks together, never venturing too far from the cabin and always as a group. But I move between the men, finding time to talk to each of them, getting to know them better in small increments. Thankfully, my newfound level of comfort with them makes me a slightly less awkward conversationalist than before, and the low-level panic that was my constant companion for so long bleeds away slowly. Even my nightmares are growing less intense.

I'm not the only one who's growing more relaxed either. The men seem to have buried the hatchet, at least somewhat. They're no longer always tense and glaring at one another as if they're in competition. They've come to a truce, with me at the center of it.

On the sixth day after Dare's addition to our little group, Ridge walks into the living room after dinner. The sun is setting, its last rays filling the cabin with a soft orange light, and it catches his silhouette perfectly as he stands near the couch, waggling something in his hand.

"Look what I found."

I have to force my attention away from his handsome face, and when I get a look at what he's holding, my brows scrunch up. "Cards?"

"Yup." His gaze darts to the men who are gathered around me on the couch and chair. "What do you say? Poker?"

"Fuck, yes." Trystan gives a cocky smile, looking pleased.

Uncle Clint used to have his buddies over for poker sometimes, and I had a love/hate relationship with those game nights. I liked them because they usually gave me an evening of respite from my uncle. But most of his friends were creepy and gross, and on nights when Clint drank too much or lost too much money, he'd take it out on me after they left.

And it was only ever men he invited over to play, so for some reason I assume Ridge is only talking to the guys—until all four of them turn to me expectantly.

"You in?" Archer asks.

Oh. Right. Of course.

These men aren't my uncle or any of his friends. They actually want to spend time with me, and they care about what *I* want.

That simple truth hits me in the chest like a ton of

bricks, and for a moment, I'm too overwhelmed by emotion to answer.

I really don't want to start crying just because they asked me to play cards with them though; they already know I'm an emotional mess, but at some point, they're gonna start thinking I'm straight-up crazy.

So I clear my throat to buy an extra second to collect myself, then glance at Ridge. "I don't know how to play."

"Well, that's easy enough to fix." He smiles down at me, then jerks his head toward the back of the cabin. "Come on. We can use the table in the kitchen."

I get up and follow the guys into the little kitchen, a little thrill of excitement running through me. Ridge and Trystan light a few candles to keep the gathering darkness at bay while Dare and Archer give me a run-down on how poker works.

To be honest, nothing they say makes any sense to me. Archer tries to break it down into manageable pieces, but Dare keeps throwing in his own two cents, and they're using words like "big blind," "flop," and "river," none of which make any sense to me.

When they finish their explanation and find me staring at them like I'm still waiting for them to *start*, Archer chuckles. "Maybe we should play a few rounds open-handed. We can guide you through it and you can see what we're talking about."

I blink. "You'd do that? You wouldn't mind?"

"Of course not." He smiles, his blue eyes warm. "We can play that way all night. I don't think any of us really care."

I half-expect Trystan to snort at that. I saw the competitive gleam in his eye when Ridge first suggested poker, and I have a feeling he was looking forward to trying to kick the other men's asses at the game. But no objection comes, and when I glance his way, he pats the seat next to him, inviting me over.

A new wave of feeling rises in my chest. These men are all so patient with me, about big things and little things —and I know it's not because they're patient people in general.

It's because of *me*.

Because they care about me.

I still don't quite know how to handle that, and the parts of me that my uncle left battered and broken still don't quite believe it. But these four shifter men prove it through their actions day after day, and I hope someday I really can trust that this is all real.

Ridge deals the first hand, and the guys talk me through the rules and strategy as we begin to play open-handed. The things Archer and Dare were saying make a lot more sense when I can see them with my own eyes, and I ask a lot of questions, absorbing everything I can.

We play two rounds like that, and I think the men really *would* be content to play this way all night. They seem to be getting as much enjoyment out of teaching me as they do out of the game itself. Trystan grins widely as he explains what "tells" are and how to look for them, and Dare flips him off when Trystan points out that he has a terrible poker face.

It's actually kind of true. Dare can be stoic and hard-edged, and I can't always tell what he's thinking. But I rarely have a hard time guessing what he's *feeling*. He wears his emotions on his sleeve, and they radiate out from him like a palpable aura.

"Okay. I think I'm ready," I say as Archer shuffles the deck. "We can play a real round if you want."

"You sure?" He glances up at me, candlelight warming his green eyes.

"Yeah."

I grin, scooting my chair a little closer to the table. Truthfully, I'm still not sure I understand everything about this game. There are a lot of bits I'm a little fuzzy on, but I want to try playing a regular game.

"All right." Archer grins at me, then deals the cards face down.

We start to play, and I immediately realize I've made a mistake. I *thought* I had a handle on this game, but now that I'm trying to strategize on my own, I feel a little out of my depth again.

So I focus on what Trystan told me about tells and study each of the men gathered around the table with me, trying to guess whether they've got a good hand. I can at least do that, even if I don't quite remember whether *my* hand is good or bad.

They look back at me, their gazes just as penetrating as mine, and I realize with a start that this is my favorite part of the game—having an excuse to stare at these men.

The candlelight casts their faces in shadow, making them look beautiful and almost otherworldly. Archer's blond hair gleams like gold as he runs a hand through it, and Dare presses his full lips together as he contemplates whether to call or fold. Trystan's gaze slides to mine, and I can practically see the glee dancing behind his turquoise eyes.

He's having fun.

They all are. And so am I.

It's a little thing in some ways, just like their willingness to take the time to teach me. But in other ways, it's *everything*. For entire years of my life, "fun" was something foreign to me, so far outside the realm of my experience that it might as well be another language.

But right now, sitting around a table with four burly men—four wolf shifters—it feels easy.

It feels right.

I could happily spend months out here in this cabin, with nothing to do all day but cook, eat, talk, and explore the woods. Part of me wishes we could stay here forever, even though I know that's not possible. I might not have responsibilities beyond these four walls, but the men do. I can tell that all of them, even Dare, worry sometimes about the duties they're neglecting while they hole up here.

They have packs that rely on them, and once my wolf finally appears and makes her choice, this blissful little bubble will burst and reality will come flooding back in.

It will happen sooner or later. I know it will.

Nothing this good can last forever.

But as I glance around the table at my four companions, narrowing my eyes in mock suspicion as I hold my cards close to my face, I wonder how on earth my wolf will ever choose.

How can she, when *I* can't?

THE SUN IS SETTING over the mountains, already casting a purple twilight over the cabin.

It's hunting time.

Since Dare's arrival at the cabin nine days ago, he's joined the hunting party every night. I get the sense that he likes spending time as a wolf, that he *needs* it, almost. A break from the stresses and strains of being a human, I guess. I don't know.

Archer gives me a sweet kiss on the cheek, and Trystan taps my nose with his finger, grinning at the way I scrunch up my face at him. Dare's gaze lingers on me before he joins the other two in the yard.

"Don't be gone too long," I say.

"We'll be back before you know it," Trystan promises, before giving me a wicked smile and shoving his shorts to his ankles.

A hot flush rises in my neck, and I fight the urge to fan myself as all three men disrobe in the front yard. Before I can fall into the trap of looking at things I shouldn't be, they shimmer with the magic of the change. A moment later, three large wolves dash off into the forest to find dinner.

I've started to love watching them shift, but in the same breath, I feel... envious. Shifting is this beautiful, magical thing that seems incredibly out of my reach.

I find Ridge in the kitchen, chopping carrots on a beat-up cutting board while a pot of water boils on the wood stove. I love watching him cook. Where Archer is lively and talkative about cooking, Ridge goes silent and contemplative, working with an impressive precision. The two of them have made every meal a delicious experience.

His posture shifts a little as soon as I walk into the room, the same way it always does. These men are so attuned to me that it sometimes feels like they're *attached* to me somehow, like some kind of invisible cord connects us at all times.

He glances over his shoulder with an easy smile and points at the counter behind me. "Want to cut potatoes?"

"Sure." I grab the mesh bag he's indicated and carry it across the kitchen to his side. There's only one cutting board, but luckily it's a big one, so I grab another knife and set to work halving the potatoes to throw in the pot. I don't mind being so close to him. In fact, I love it. I crave it.

The need to be near them has grown from a subtle impulse to an undeniable, constant pull over the course of our time here, and I've given up fighting it.

They're all careful to avoid pushing me too far—even Dare, although I feel the memories of our first meeting hovering over nearly every interaction we have—so I haven't kissed any of them since the day Trystan pressed his lips to mine in this very kitchen.

But they let me touch them all I like. They encourage it even, and I can practically feel how it soothes them the same way it soothes me.

It awakens something in me too. A heat and a need that refuses to be satisfied with little touches and chaste kisses.

That feeling still isn't drawing me toward one of the men over the others though, and it's starting to make me question my willpower and my sanity.

They told me. These men and the elders—they all told me that my wolf would choose.

So why hasn't she?

Where *is* she?

Those thoughts swirl through my head as I work beside Ridge. Our elbows touch as we chop, and I can feel the warmth rolling off his skin.

We continue our dinner prep in silence for a few minutes, though he keeps shooting glances at me, his brow furrowed. He always seems to know when something's weighing on me. I don't know if I'm just that easy to read, or if Ridge has a stronger intuition than anyone I've ever met.

Finally, he asks, "What's wrong?"

"How do you know something's wrong?" I toss two halves of a potato into the pot of water with a soft splash.

He puts down his knife and turns to face me, one eyebrow lifting. "Is there not?"

Letting out a sigh, I put my own knife down and shrug. "I don't know. I guess I'm just worried the elder was wrong."

"About what exactly?" Ridge steps closer, reaching out to squeeze my hand.

"About me being a shifter. If I'll ever shift. Maybe I'm not really one of you," I say, voice small. Until saying it out loud, I never really gave that particular fear too much power in my mind. Now that I have, I realize I really *am* worried this is all a fluke. Maybe it's been nothing but a huge misunderstanding.

I'm not a shifter.

None of these men will ever belong to me.

All of this is just a brief moment of blissful peace and happiness, a short interlude before I'll have to figure out what to do with the rest of my life.

How to survive on my own.

But Ridge shakes his head adamantly, his other hand lifting to touch my chest, right over my heart. "You're wrong about that, sweetheart. She's in there. I can feel her, and I know she'll come out soon."

His smile is so gentle, so kind. Just as he's been every step of the way with me.

There's something else there too, beneath that comforting relationship we've formed. The thing that always lingers between us, demanding more.

More.

Our fingers are still entwined, and his palm rests between my breasts. Amora was so generous to give me clothes for this adventure, but she only gave me *one* bra. And it's hanging over the shower curtain rod to dry after I washed it in the sink this morning.

If he moved his hand just a couple inches...

Desire swirls inside me, and I blush at my own wantonness. *Step away*, I tell myself, trying to force my feet to move, but it's too late. I watch, mesmerized, as Ridge smells the change in my body chemistry.

He stiffens, his hand hot on my chest. His pupils expand, and his lips part.

I'm too attracted to him to care that he knows my inner desires, too swept up in the heat building strong and fast inside me. I can't stop imagining his hand shifting to the right, our bodies coming together, and dammit, I want him to make the first move because I'm a coward.

But he won't. I know he won't, because he's Ridge.

He's a *good* man.

Too good.

It's that thought that unsticks my feet from the floor. He is good, and that's why I'm coming to care for him so much. But right now I want him to let go of that goodness, that protective worry he has for me, just a little bit.

I want to be bad. And I want him to join me.

I take a small step toward him, angling my body just enough that his hand slides over my breast. The moment he realizes I'm braless, his expression darkens with unfiltered desire.

"Sable..." He mutters gruffly, letting my name trail off. I love the sound of my name on his lips.

Arching my back, I close my eyes against the way the fabric bunches around his fingers, scraping over my nipple. Ridge hasn't moved a muscle, even as my nipple pebbles beneath his fingertips. There's something in his expression that says he's just as surprised at my behavior as I am.

Suddenly, his fingers tighten over my swollen nipple, and I gasp at the way the pinch goes straight to the wet heat between my legs. Ridge curses, his nostrils flaring.

And then his lips crash into mine.

This kiss isn't as frantic as the one I shared with Dare on the bank of the stream, but it's just as consuming. I go hot in his arms as he shoves me back against the kitchen counter, grinding his hips against mine. His hands move lower and then he lifts me onto the counter, opening my legs around his hips.

My arms wrap around his neck as I clutch at him a little desperately, my legs hooking around his waist like I'm trying to pin our bodies together. To bind us so closely nothing can pull us apart.

I've been wanting to do this for longer than I could ever admit. I've *needed* this for fucking days.

His lips part, and his tongue dances with mine as his hands slide beneath my shirt. When he cups my bare breasts with his calloused hands, I moan into his kiss, my head whirling from the rush of adrenaline and arousal in my veins.

After several moments, he pulls away, both his hands emerging from beneath my shirt to cup my face. He looks into my eyes, breathing heavily, his own cheeks flushed.

God, I like him like this. I love the sight of him coming a little bit undone, and I love knowing that I'm the one who made him that way.

This massive, powerful, controlled man wants me.

Needs me.

And I need him too.

"Ridge, I..." My tongue darts out to lick my lips, tasting the addictive flavor of him on my skin. I don't know quite what I want to say, what I want to ask for, but I hope he can understand.

The wolf shifter's amber eyes almost seem to glow in the fading light. He opens his mouth to speak when a soft noise comes from behind the cabin.

He goes tense, his gaze darting to the back door.

"Do you think they're already back?" I ask, confused by his reaction. If it were only Trystan, Archer, and Dare outside, I don't think he'd look so ready to fight. My skin prickles with unease.

Ridge's senses are on full alert. Even in human form, he looks like a wolf, with his nose in the air and his eyes unfocused as he listens to sounds well outside my range of hearing. "No. I don't think so. That's not anyone I know."

Fear strikes a chord within me, and I fight the urge to run. "A stranger?"

Ridge catches my frightened gaze and briefly touches my face, then murmurs, "Stay here."

Before I can argue, he leaves me sitting on the counter and disappears through the back door into the darkening night.

I clutch the counter beside my legs and feel that old hysteria rising up inside me. I never fully realized how calm and normal my time here at the cabin has become, but it's obvious now. My panic attacks have become so few and far between that they don't feel real anymore. The cabin has turned into a safe place, somewhere I can be me without fear of abuse or judgment.

But now there's something here that doesn't fit that narrative.

No sounds emerge from behind the cabin. Ridge closed the door behind him. I'm sure he did it because he wanted to protect me, but I don't like not being able to hear what's happening. What if he's in danger? I glance at the counter where our two knives are lying by the cutting board. If all else fails, at least I have a weapon. Of sorts.

The clock on the wall ticks loudly in the silence, counting each second since Ridge walked out. I strain to hear anything beyond the cabin walls, wishing I had the preternatural senses of a shifter.

It's okay, Sable. It's probably nothing.

I repeat the comforting words to myself, trying to believe them. Trying not to let my old fears run away with me.

Any moment, Ridge will probably walk back through the door with a grin, telling me he found possums in the trash.

But I know that's not the case. Ridge didn't smell an animal outside. He smelled a person. *"That's not anyone I know."*

A loud pop breaks the mountain silence, and I jump, toppling off the counter in my shock. I've heard gunfire before, back when Clint and his friends would drink too much and go out to shoot Coke bottles in the yard, and I'm almost positive that's what just came from behind the cabin.

My heart seizes in my chest.

Ridge.

A wave of fear and adrenaline like I've never known

surges through me, so powerful it feels like I got struck by lightning.

Not Ridge. No.

Nothing can happen to the large, serious man who's my protector, my savior, since the very first moment I met him. It can't. I won't let it.

I reach for the biggest of the two knives with trembling fingers, my heart racing as though it's trying to beat a hole in my sternum. Who knows how much good it will do. It's not like a knife could do any good in a gunfight, but the weight of it in my hand steadies my nerves.

Could the witches have found us?

Maybe that sound wasn't a gunshot at all, but the sound of something magical, some kind of spell that knocked him out.

Or killed him, the terrified part of my mind suggests darkly.

My knife won't do any good against magic either.

In this moment, that hardly matters though. The thought of Ridge out there, alone and in trouble, is enough to send me darting toward the back door, spurred on by the primal need to keep him safe.

I'm halfway down the hall when the door swings open. But instead of Ridge, another familiar face appears in my vision as a man strides inside, blasting apart the safety and comfort of this cabin.

Uncle Clint.

"Found you, you little shit," he snarls, then stalks toward me.

Everything inside me screams at me to react, but terror has turned me to ice. For a second, it's as if the past two weeks never happened. It's as if I never stepped foot outside of Uncle Clint's truck that night, never dared to step out of line.

For a second, I'm nothing but the scared little girl he beat and abused for years just because he could.

It's my fear for Ridge that brings me back from that place. Fear for the man I've come to care for that reminds me these two weeks *did* happen—that I'm not the same girl I was.

As Clint nears me, I lash out with the knife, slicing wildly toward him. My movement is jerky, but I don't think he was expecting it, because I manage to catch the edge of his arm with the tip of the blade. The sharp knife tears through his flannel shirt before biting into skin, and he hisses in pain, jerking back.

An ugly look crosses his face, and he charges forward, blood dripping from the gash in his arm.

Before I can slash again, he grabs me by the arm, his fingers hard and bruising, and bats the knife away from my hand with his gun. Sharp pain cracks across my knuckles as the gun makes contact, and my only means of protecting myself skitters away over the kitchen floor, little droplets of blood flying from the blade.

"You little cunt. Thought you got all tough out here in the fuckin' woods, huh? Did your boyfriend teach you that?" he snarls.

However deep I managed to cut his arm, it clearly wasn't deep enough. His grip is strong as he hauls me into a headlock, pinning my back to his chest. Then he drags me toward the door, the barrel of the gun pressed to my temple.

I've lost the ability to move my feet, and I collapse against his grip on my arm, my legs dragging uselessly on the floor. This is the culmination of every nightmare I've had since running away from him, the thing I told myself would never happen. *Could* never happen.

Maybe I should've known better.

I hold out hope that Ridge is outside, that Clint didn't shoot him dead, and when we emerge, he'll be waiting to tear my uncle's throat out.

But that hope is ripped to shreds when Clint drags me out over the cool grass and into the night—past Ridge's limp, still body.

27

TRYSTAN

I NEVER THOUGHT I'd enjoy hunting with shifters outside my pack, but these dumb fucks actually make it enjoyable.

I've known Archer for most of my life, though not in any kind of familiar context. Just as that dude who's dad is the dying alpha of the East Pack and who probably isn't strong enough to take the mantle when the old man croaks.

But he surprises me when we're on the hunt. I had little doubt before that Dare was just as strong and skilled as me, but Archer is too. We work together like a well-oiled machine, evenly matched and able to anticipate each other's moves.

I fly over the undergrowth into position, forming a third point on our triangle around the herd of grazing deer. There are five of them to choose from, all with their noses in the grass in a small field, completely oblivious to the threat surrounding them. Whoever can't run fast enough is going to be dinner.

The wind carries me Dare's scent, and I can see Archer just beyond the shadow of fading sunlight. We're in place. Excitement courses through my veins, and I let out a barely audible yip. As one, the three of us leap forward.

The deer scatter on our approach. As we crash into the clearing, they panic and try to find an opening to run, to escape us before we can take them down. We rush around them, growling and snapping, and the stronger deer make their escape.

That's okay, because we aren't there for the strongest, fastest deer. Once they're in flight, the one we want is well behind and not capable of fleeing. The fastest deer get to live another day; the slowest gets to feed a bunch of hungry shifters.

Dare reaches our prey first and takes her down with a well-placed leap and a snap of his jaws. Within moments, her blood is cooling on the grass and her companions are long gone.

The circle of fucking life.

If we were out here for funsies, we'd just rip into her as is and have ourselves a raw feast. I love hunts like that, getting my snout bloody beneath the open sky, the meat still warm as we tear into it. But we're feeding Sable too, which means taking the deer back to the cabin and tossing it on the grill. I'm not picky. I like it both ways.

We shift back and hover over the beast, eyeing our handiwork.

"Nice takedown," I tell Dare as he wipes his mouth. And I mean it.

"No better than you would have done yourself," he replies with a shrug. "Archer's strategy was the real MVP here."

Archer grins, then leans over to grab the deer's front legs. "It was a team effort. Come on, let's get this back."

I pick up the back legs, and we heft the beast up before beginning to follow our own scent trails back toward the cabin. Conversation between us comes a lot easier now than it did a few days ago. I don't know that I'd call them friends, exactly, but I feel a lot less animosity toward them than I once did.

All because of a sexy little blonde who owns each and every one of my thoughts.

The generator is on in the cabin, so we see the lights from the windows through the trees before we see the building itself. The steady *thwump thwump* of the generator purring at the side of the structure is an out of place white noise on the silent night. I'm not a fan of the thing, since it inhibits our ability to hear properly outside the cabin. If witches were to find a way onto North Pack territory, they could sneak up on us when that thing's going, and we might not be the wiser until it was too late. It's a hazard, and I've said so.

But light is one of the few things that keeps Sable's darkness at bay, so every night without fail, we turn on the generator. Her comfort is paramount. To all of us.

We're just beyond the tree line when alarm bells start ringing in my head. At the same instant, Dare and Archer stiffen beside me, their noses turning to the air.

"Something's wrong," Dare growls.

"A stranger," Archer adds, turning his wide eyes on me.

We both let go of the deer in the same instant, letting it drop to the ground behind us as we break into a run.

Our footsteps pound over the undergrowth as we rush to the cabin. My heart's pounding wildly, a savage thing in my chest. All I can think of is Sable, getting to her and finding her safe.

My stomach drops when we come across Ridge's body lying prone in the backyard, while the back door stands open to the night.

Archer kneels beside Ridge's form and checks his pulse, then gently turns his head to expose an oblong object poking from his neck. He tugs it out of Ridge's skin and holds it up to the light.

"Fuck. A tranquilizer." His voice is stark with fear as he looks up at the house.

Dare and I both rush inside at once, nearly getting jammed in the goddamn doorway as we race into the kitchen.

It's empty.

He heads toward the front of the cabin while I sweep the bedroom and bathroom. When he meets me back in the hallway, I can tell by the devastation on his face that Sable is gone.

"Nothing." His voice sounds dead, blank almost, like he has to turn off every emotion inside him just to get the damn word out.

"Fuck. *Fuck*."

I could punch a hole through the wall. I could tear this cabin down with my bare hands right now. But neither of those things would get us closer to getting Sable back, and that's the only thing that matters right now.

She's the only thing that matters.

I jerk my chin toward the door, and the two of us rush back out into the night.

Outside, Archer is helping a woozy Ridge sit up. I'm surprised at the rush of relief I feel that he's okay. Although we've never been enemies, I wouldn't have called us friends either until recently. But I'm thankful as fuck that he's not dead.

Ridge groans, rubbing the back of his neck where Archer yanked the dart out. "Someone snuck up on me. I heard a noise out here, and I came to check it out..." He trails off and looks up, his eyes so wide I can see the whites all the way around. "Sable?"

"She's gone," I tell him, my voice rough as fucking gravel.

Ridge launches to his feet so fast he almost keels right back over, but Archer grabs him and steadies him.

"We have to find her." Ridge shakes his head, looking half-drunk as his body fights off the tranquilizers in his system. "I didn't like the smell of this guy. Fucking sociopath."

"You don't think her uncle..." Archer lets the half-formed question die out.

Fury blooms through me, and I snarl.

Yes. I *do* think. Witches wouldn't have used a fucking tranq gun, they would've used magic. "We have to find her."

As one, the four of us immediately shift back to our wolf forms. Ridge is unsteady on his feet, but he gives himself a good shake and pushes Archer's golden wolf away as he tries to help.

You're too drugged to go with us, I tell him. *Don't be an idiot. Go lie down.*

I'm going, Ridge snaps back.

Dare puts his head down near the edge of the cabin's clearing, sniffing the ground erratically. Then he stiffens, his hackles rising and his nose turning into the wind. His howl pierces the night, and then we're all racing after him.

We fly through the shadowy forest, following Sable's scent and the scent of the man who took her. I can tell where she gave up walking and he picked her up to carry her through the woods. Where there were once two scent trails, there's suddenly only one on the ground, with Sable just a hint on the air, already dying away.

Just the thought of that man's hands on her makes me see red. My jaws itch to rip his throat out.

I'll fucking destroy him.

The trail takes us out of the woods and onto a small, dirt service trail. These exist throughout the mountains, placed here by the government or by thrill seekers looking to have an adventure in the wilderness. The wolf packs typically avoid them—out of sight, out of mind, and all that. The last thing we need is a thrill seeking hiker with a GoPro on his helmet catching footage of a shifter transforming.

But the scent trail ends at fresh tire tracks. The fucker put Sable in a car and took off with her.

Archer speaks up in my mind. *A big white farmhouse on the outskirts of Big Creek. That's what she said.*

Ridge nods once. *It's about twenty miles from here.*

Dare shakes himself. *You know where we're going?*

I do, Ridge says.

Then lead the way, I tell him, ready to follow him to the ends of the earth to save her. *We've got your back.*

The moon is rising over the mountains as we settle into a full-on sprint, following Ridge on a straight line for more populated areas.

Fear eats me alive. I never knew I could be so attached to someone, but Sable is one of the fiercest, sweetest creatures I've ever met.

And there's not a chance in hell I'll let anything happen to her.

28

SABLE

When I open my eyes, there's a steady throbbing in my head that makes me think I might explode.

I can place the origin for the pain too. I remember seeing my uncle's jacked-up truck sitting on a dirt road several miles beyond the cabin. At the sight of it, adrenaline pumped through me and turned me crazy. I knew without a doubt if I let him put me in that truck, I was as good as dead. So I kicked and punched and screamed as if my life depended on it, which it likely did.

Unfortunately, my uncle's never been one to be squeamish about silencing my screams.

I saw his gun hurtling toward my temple, and that's the last thing I remember beyond flashes of a hard floor and the rumble of his truck as he drove me away from my only means of protection.

They'll never find me.

I fight back tears, because I refuse to give in to this situation. Clint won't break me. I won't fucking let him. I'll fight like he's never seen before—I'll scream and claw and do whatever I can to hurt him before he kills me.

I recognize the four cold concrete walls around me. The antique metal Bud Light sign hanging by a long, narrow window filled with thick glass. The work bench along the wall covered in tools he rarely touched, and the paint canisters covered in a layer of dust. I know this basement all too well, as the place where I was punished when he felt like I needed an extra heavy hand.

I'm on my side, facing the work bench with the vises he's used on me more than once. My arms are tied in front of me with duct tape, but he didn't bother with my legs. The realization sends me reeling.

How many times have I just let him hurt me? How often did I just lie there and take it, to make him think I don't need to be fully tied up now?

How broken does he think I am?

A thick work boot stomps into view, followed by the second. His boots are looking a bit worse for the wear, like he's been too busy beating the shit out of me to care about the state of his shoes.

"So this is the thanks I get?" Uncle Clint grunts.

I roll onto my back so that I can see his face. Not because I care to lock eyes with the man who hurt me for so long, but because I can't glare at him with the full extent of hatred in my soul if I'm staring at his boots.

"This is the thanks I get for raising your useless ass," he goes on, glaring down at me. The arm I sliced is wrapped in a heavy white bandage, and the sight of it gives me a grim sort of satisfaction. "You running away. Takin' off in the middle of the road like that, makin' me chase after you. I just tore the countryside apart to find you, you stupid bitch."

I ignore his final slur and focus on the words that send a harsh laugh bursting up my throat.

"Raising me?" The words don't even feel real as they trip off my tongue. "If you 'raised me,' that would imply you did something *good* for my well-being. And you've never been good to me a day in your life."

Uncle Clint stares at me for a long moment, shock clear on his weathered face. I've never talked back to him like this. Usually, his long rants are just met by silence from me, because I know anything I say will only piss him off more.

But right now, I don't care.

Clint's lip curls, an ugly sneer contorting his features. Then he drops to his knees with a lot more ease than a man his age and weight should have. He backhands me so hard that stars fill my vision, and I struggle to suck in air around the pain. He grabs my taped hands and pins them to my chest. With his other hand, he tugs the knife from his pocket and flips it open.

No!

I refuse to let him hurt me anymore. I'm not the girl I once was. I'm *not*. I was able to run away from him, to rise above my fear and get the hell out. I won't be defaulting to my old ways, where I just closed my eyes and took whatever punishment he meted out.

Fuck. No.

I buck wildly, yanking my wrists out of his hand. He reaches for me again, brandishing the knife, but I lean into his legs and nail him in the junk with an elbow.

Clint yowls, falling sideways and dropping the knife in the process. As he hits the concrete, I roll over onto my knees and start crawling away, moving at a snail's pace thanks to my duct taped hands.

He recuperates too fast. One meaty fist reaches into my hair and drags me back toward him.

But I won't go down without a fight. I will shred him to pieces with every last breath in my body, even if I still die in the end.

I refuse to cower in fear anymore.

Suddenly, a chorus of howls reach my ears. My stomach flips over at the haunting noise, and relief surges through me in a rush. There's no other sound in the world right now that could bring me so much joy.

"What the fuck..."

Clint mutters a curse under his breath. He still has me by the hair, and I'm on my knees clutching the hem of his shirt to try to take some of the pressure off my scalp. I can't see his face from my vantage point, but I wish I could.

I wish I could see his expression when four massive wolves burst into his basement.

My shifter companions are the most beautiful sight I've ever seen as they hurtle down the stairs and across the cement floor. They look magnificent and predatory, their teeth bared and their sights set on my uncle.

Clint lets go of my hair with an almost feminine shriek, and I collapse onto the concrete. I take the full force of my weight with my shoulder, grunting from the pain. My scalp is on fire from the way he slung me around, which probably means I lost a good chunk of hair. But I'll take a few bald spots if it means I walk out of this alive.

Before Clint can reach for me again, I barrel roll away from him. The wolves are charging toward him with jaws snapping, and I don't want to get in their way as they leap for him. My legs flail and my arms gain some new bruises as I roll across the floor, everything spinning in my vision.

A gunshot ricochets through the basement, and my heart crashes against my ribs as I come to a stop against the workbench.

Fuck. He's shooting at them.

The shifters are powerful, but they're not invincible. He could kill them if he gets in a good shot.

Scrambling to my knees, I watch as Ridge's light brown wolf latches onto Clint's arm. Clint cries out, his fingers jolting from the pain, and the gun slips from his grasp. Archer darts in to bat it away, while Dare and Trystan lunge to take the old man down.

Clint is undeterred. He tears away from Ridge's teeth, taking a hunk of skin out of his arm in the process, and then stumbles away. Black-furred Dare manages to grab Clint's blue jeans and take him to the floor, but Clint draws his knife and swipes out, making all four wolves dart away.

He gets back to his feet and kicks out wildly, catching Ridge in the face. He shoves at the growling, snapping wolves one more time before rushing across the basement toward the empty room where he used to keep me for "time out." He manages to slide into the small, narrow stone room and jam the door shut.

My wolf companions throw themselves at the door. They're monstrous, nothing but strength and muscle, and I think if given the time, they'd crack the heavy door down like it was made of plaster.

But they aren't given a chance.

A moment after Clint walls up inside, a siren wails in the distance, and even I can tell it's steadily drawing closer.

"The cops are coming!" I shout, struggling against the duct tape on my wrists. "We have to get out of here. They're all dirty and friends with Clint."

Not to mention, *any* cop—dirty or not—would be likely to shoot what they'd see as feral wolves.

Archer's golden wolf falls away from the door and lopes to my side. Magic shimmers over him until he's human again, and he quickly rips through the duct tape to free my hands. His handsome, boy-next-door face is pained as he helps me to my feet.

"Did he hurt you?" He cups my cheeks, green eyes searching my face.

I shake my head. "No. Not like before."

Pain flashes in his eyes, but he just leans forward and kisses me. "Let's get out of here. Climb on my back."

Before I can respond, he shimmers with the change once again. He gives a short, sharp bark, and the other three wolves finally leave the door behind which my uncle is hiding.

Then we run from the house, the wolves dashing up the stairs single file as I cling with all my might to Archer's fur.

The sirens grow louder as we burst out into the cool night air, and the wolves wheel in the opposite direction of the noise, paws thundering over the ground as they run flat-out.

I don't look back. Not once. I don't want to see the white house that holds too many of my nightmares.

I hope to God that was the last time I ever have to see that awful place.

29
SABLE

ARCHER MOVES SWIFTLY and gracefully beneath me as we race out of town. I clutch his fur and keep my head down, though I can't help but steal glances at our surroundings as we run.

I don't know this place, even though I lived here my whole life. My whole world was narrowed down to the house I was kept in, where each room might as well have been its own continent and my only real connection to the outside world were the books and movies I occasionally got my hands on.

We pass a barber shop, a movie theater, and a bank, the latter of which is obviously closed for the night. The buildings are old but well kept, mostly stone and connected by alleyways, and there are planters full of flowers everywhere. Everything is so *normal*, like a quaint little movie set used for a romantic comedy.

How did I come to live my own personal horror in a town this cute?

I gasp as I see people coming out of a corner grocery, talking and laughing among themselves in the light pouring from the windows. A group of teens carrying soda bottles and cigarette packs. Every single one of their jaws drop at the sight of the four giant wolves racing down Main Street.

Fuck.

Burying my face in Archer's golden fur, I focus on taking a couple of deep breaths. I've come this far without a panic attack; I refuse to give in now. It can't be good that people are seeing me and the men like this. Shifters have stayed hidden for so long on purpose, to protect themselves from human fear.

But... my wolves came for me anyway.

It still doesn't feel real. I don't know how Clint found me in that remote cabin, but it doesn't matter. Because all four of the shifters came to save me. Thank God I opened up to them about my life and told them about where I was raised. Regardless, I have a feeling they would have found me even if they had to tear apart the countryside piece by piece.

They came for me.

I recall standing on the edge of Ridge's village, weighing my options after I raced away from the elder's shack. Archer promised me that if I stayed, if I went to the cabin with them to give the mate bond a chance, I would be the safest I could possibly be.

He obviously didn't lie either.

Because they came for me.

The thought keeps repeating over and over in my head like a mantra. I grip Archer's fur tighter, pressing my face into his neck. I relish the power of his body beneath me, and how his scent is wild and musky. He's panting loud enough that I can hear him over the thundering of his giant paws, but he doesn't slow. None of the men slow down as we leave the village behind and disappear into the wilderness.

These four men will protect me no matter what.

Time passes. We run so far and so long that my legs grow tired from clenching around Archer's ribcage, and my fingers get weak from gripping his fur. By the time we slow to a stop, the moon is high in the sky and the inky blackness above is dotted with a million pinpricks of light.

I raise my head from Archer's neck to find the now-familiar mating cabin visible between the trees ahead of us. It looks calm and serene in the dark night, like a place of safety and solace.

God, I hope that's what it is.

Would my uncle come back here? Would he try again to find me and drag me back home after seeing what he just saw. I have to hope his sense of self-preservation is strong enough that he won't want to fuck with the four massive wolves who invaded his home.

And if he does come looking for me again, I hope the men kill him.

I wish they'd killed him already.

Now that we're no longer running, a chill sets into my bones. I came so close to dying today. I had allowed myself to believe that I was free of my uncle for good. Every day I spent in that cabin with these men healed me just that little bit, and in the blink of an eye, my uncle sliced open the safety net.

Will I ever really be safe as long as he's alive?

Wrapping my arms around myself, I focus on my breathing like Archer taught me. The shock of ending up back at Clint's, and the trauma of facing him again, aren't going to pass easily. I'm shaking like a leaf and colder than I should be. The adrenaline dump, I guess.

The lights are off inside the cabin as we approach, and Dare fires up the generator. He murmurs something to Ridge as we all head inside the cabin, and the amber-eyed shifter answers in a low voice.

Oh, God. Ridge.

The reminder of the last time I saw him in human form tears through me like a bomb. As soon as we're inside the front door and Trystan turns on the light, I throw myself at Ridge with tears pooling in my eyes.

His arms wrap around me automatically, and I bury

my face in his chest. I can hardly speak through the lump in my throat. "I thought you were dead."

His voice is rough, and his thick arms tighten around me. "No, sweetheart, not dead. Just got tranqued. I can't believe that fucker got the drop on me."

Our companions are still close by, but I can hear them murmuring to one another in low voices—giving me and Ridge the moment we need. This man has saved my life more than once now, and I'll be forever indebted to him for that.

But more importantly...

I breathe in his pine scent and revel in the warmth of his bare skin against my own. That delicious scent eases my panic. From the first day I awoke in his bed, his scent felt like coming home, and that's more true now than ever.

I wish I could comfort him the same way he's comforting me. There's still tension in his body, and it turns his muscles hard and rigid even as his hands slide soothingly over my back.

"Are you okay?" I ask, my voice barely a whisper. I pull back and tilt my head up to look into his eyes.

Ridge slides a hand around from my back to cup my face. His thumb plays across my jaw as he stares down at me, his dark eyes full of emotion. "Fuck. No, little wolf. I'm scared of losing you."

"You didn't lose me. You *found* me," I point out with a small smile. But the look on his face has set my heart into a dizzying pace. My own fear and emotions churning inside me have been threatening to take me down since the moment Clint walked through the cabin door.

I remember the way Ridge held me in the shower as the water washed over us both. Just held me with no expectations of me, no irritation at how long it took me to learn to breathe again. He's been caring for me since the moment he picked me up off the canyon floor, when he could have left me there.

He hasn't *had* to do any of this. He's chosen to. Again and again and again, he's chosen to protect me. Chosen to care for me.

Chosen *me*.

I move my hand up his chest, my fingers tracing over the muscles of his torso. His breath hitches in his throat, and his gaze drops to my lips. With just those two small things, need rises inside me.

Heat flashes over my skin and fills the air between us. Before I can second-guess it or overthink it, I wrap my arms around him and rise up onto my tiptoes to kiss him.

It's as if the last several hours never took place.

Or maybe it's like this *because* of the last several hours. Because we both know what we almost lost.

Suddenly, we're kissing like we did earlier in the kitchen, with barely controlled abandon.

Ridge grips my hips and pulls me against him, reminding me that he's fully naked. As our kiss deepens, he hardens against my belly, and the sensation sends a thrill of reckless desire through me. I undulate against him and catch his surprised gasp with my lips. He moves a hand lower, grabbing my ass and tugging me against him, while his other hand slips beneath my shirt to palm my breast. His thumb lingers over my nipple, and I feel a tug between my legs as if both parts of me are somehow connected.

The flames burning through my blood rise higher and higher. I lose all sense of myself and all sense of our surroundings as Ridge thoroughly explores my mouth with his tongue. I can't even think through the heat, through the need. My body is burning for his touch to be everywhere all at once.

I break away, gasping. I'm lightheaded, so hot there's nothing in the world that could cool me down.

Something I've never felt before is rising up inside me.

Something is happening to me.

30

DARE

JEALOUSY BURNS like fire inside me as I watch Sable kiss Ridge. It's not a sweet, chaste kiss—it's the kind of carnal embrace that comes before a man buries himself to the hilt inside a woman and relishes the moan he elicits when he bottoms out inside her. The exact thing I've been imagining since the night I found Sable on the edge of the creek looking like moonlight come to life.

I clench my fists at my side and glare, my wolf growling and protesting without making a sound.

That should be *me*.

I wish like fuck it *was* me pressed against her, tasting her lips, my hands on her body. I'm half-tempted to rip Ridge away from her and take his place.

She's *mine*, my beast snarls, fighting to get loose. *Mine*.

But I remain standing just inside the front door to the cabin, my muscles locked and rigid. I'm not here for a pissing contest. I'm here to take care of my mate—to take care of Sable—and if this is what she needs, then I won't let anything in the world keep her from having this. Not even my own emotions or the chemical desire inside me demanding I take what's mine and fuck everybody else.

Suddenly, she pulls away, gasping for air. Her hands clutch at Ridge's bare chest, and she gulps in breath after breath, her eyes wild, her gaze darting around the room as if she's disoriented. Her lips are red and swollen from Ridge's kisses.

"I feel—" She cuts off, shoving her mass of satin blonde hair away from her shoulders. Her skin is pink and a sheen of perspiration lines her temple. She lets out a low, helpless noise, still gulping air.

I can almost feel the heat rolling off her body from across the foyer.

"I feel... strange," she says, the words coming out breathless and raw. "I need... something."

"What do you need?" Ridge asks in a low voice, cupping her shoulders. I'm surprised at how calm he sounds. If I were in his place, I'd be nothing but wolf, shaking with the need to complete the mating. Shit, I'm not even the one who just had my tongue down her throat, and I *am* shaking with that need.

"I-I don't know." Sable closes her eyes and leans into him, breathing deeply. Then her eyes flutter open and they've darkened, her pupils dilated as she focuses on Ridge's face.

The scent of her wraps around me. It's something so familiar that I've come to love and crave, even as I've kept my distance and respected her boundaries over our time together at the cabin.

In the blink of an eye, that familiar scent changes.

It becomes darker, deeper, headier, swirling through the room like a tornado. My body reacts instantly—warmth flashes over my skin and my cock stiffens as if she's touched it.

Fuck. She's going into heat.

I know it as sure as I know I'd give anything to be in Ridge's place right now.

Sable leans back into Ridge, kissing him with more wildness and abandon than before. Their desire becomes a living thing, and I grab the wall as it makes me lightheaded with need. I can't stop watching her in his arms, the way she moves against him, the little sounds that come from within her as she grinds against his body.

She's strung out with arousal, delirious in her quest to mate with Ridge.

To mate with him.

To complete the bond.

Goddammit.

The full realization of what that means hits me like a blow to the gut. It's done. She's chosen him.

The three of them all brought Sable up to this cabin to give her wolf space and time to choose. And after I scented her in the woods and my wolf made the same claim theirs had, I joined this little party, getting to know Sable as the five of us formed a strange, motley little band.

But if I'm being fucking honest, it never once occurred to me that she might not choose me in the end.

That's how fucking sure I was of my feelings, of the truth of this bond.

I was wrong. Her wolf has chosen Ridge as her mate. And there's not a damn thing I can do about it.

I look at Archer and Trystan, both standing off to my left. They're watching the scene with the same kind of open, bleeding pain I'm sure shows clearly on my face. They've come to the same conclusion I have.

Archer is the first to move, clenching his jaw as he blinks back what looks like honest to fuck tears in his eyes. He grabs Trystan's arm and motions with his head that we should leave the cabin.

I know he's right. Ridge has Sable pressed into the wall, one of her legs wrapped around his bare ass, and I'm not a dumbass. What comes next isn't for the three of us to stand around and watch. Sable has made her choice. No matter how much it hurts, we have to respect that.

But God-fucking-dammit, I don't want to.

It doesn't matter that her wolf hasn't chosen me. Mine has chosen her, so fully and completely that it feels like it might tear me apart. The wolf in me still howls brokenly in my soul, torn between two competing impulses—to protect Sable, and to claim her.

I can't do both. Protecting her heart means walking away.

Even if it fucking kills me to do it.

Archer's hand is on the door handle when Sable cries, "No! Stop!"

All three of us turn around to find her a couple feet away from Ridge, who's collecting himself against the wall in her absence. She takes a tentative step forward, those big blue eyes wide, her long lashes blinking away a cloud of unreserved lust.

I've never seen her look more beautiful or powerful than she is right now. I want to bow down at her feet and fucking worship her.

"Don't go," she murmurs, still breathing hard. "I can't let you go. I need you. All of you. Please."

The crack in her voice tears through me, and I take an involuntary step toward her in response, drawn to her by a magnetic force. But I stop, hesitating for a long moment.

What she's saying... what she's asking for...

It never occurred to me that we could share her. Sharing isn't something coded into us. It's not something shifters do, and it's definitely not something I do with much of *anything* in my life. I'm solitary for a reason. I'm a grouchy motherfucker who doesn't like sharing what's his.

Behind me, Trystan and Archer seem to be warring with the same thoughts and feelings. I don't sense either of them moving, only the waves of confusion rolling off them as we all take in the beautiful woman before us.

"Please stay," Sable says, her voice husky. As she continues speaking, she meets my gaze, then does the same with each of the shifters behind me. "Something is happening to me. It's—I need you. Not just one of you. *All of you.*"

And that does it.

That breaks me.

Just as there isn't a chance in hell I'd ever stand in the way of something Sable desires, I'd never deny her either. So I stride across the small expanse between us and step up to her, reaching out to touch her face. Behind her, Ridge joins me, one of his hands curling around her belly. Her need rises immediately, the scent of her desire like a drug racing across my senses.

Trystan and Archer are right behind me, taking their places on either side of us until the four of us surround her.

This is not at all how I imagined this would go, but as I gaze into Sable's perfect gray-blue eyes, I realize it doesn't really matter. Because she needs this.

And I'd do anything I can to make her happy.

Cupping her chin, I tilt her head up a bit more as I drop my own, and when our lips meet, I can *taste* the way her desire has changed her body chemistry. She tastes sweeter, wilder than she did the first time we kissed, and it makes my hard cock pulse with a fresh shock of arousal.

She groans into my mouth, sliding her tongue against mine as her breath picks up. I can feel her moving, her ass grinding against Ridge behind her as our kiss deepens. She undulates her hips, shifting between the two of us as she seeks more relief from the heat building inside her.

Ridge lets out a choked grunt as her perfect ass rubs against his cock again, and the sound stokes something inside me. He can feel her response to me in the urgency of her movements, and it makes an unexpected swell of pride and lust rise up in me. Good. I *want* him to feel it. I want all these men to know how badly Sable wants me.

I kiss her harder, plundering her mouth before drawing her sweet little tongue into my own mouth and sucking on it. She whimpers softly, her breath coming in short gasps.

I'm breathing harder too, my head spinning like I'm drunk as I lose myself in the sweet perfection of her body. Her spirit. Every fucking thing there is about this beautiful, vulnerable goddess.

When our lips finally break apart, hers are even more full than usual, swollen from the punishing attention from first Ridge, then me.

Her eyelashes flutter as her tongue darts out to taste me, but before I can kiss her again, Trystan catches her chin with two fingertips and turns her head toward him, claiming her lips for himself.

An instinctual jealousy rears in my chest, my wolf scratching at my rib cage as it demands I fight him. Kill him. Destroy him.

But before I can make a move to do anything, Sable's hand slides down between us and finds my cock, her fingertips brushing over my shaft.

My eyelids droop, all thoughts of violence and killing evaporating from my head as pleasure like I've never known surges through me.

Fuck. She's so damn perfect.

Her touch is light and tentative at first, soft as a butterfly's wings, but as Trystan's greedy tongue plunders her mouth, she lets out a desperate whimper. I can tell he's driving her wild with his kiss, and she takes it out on my dick, wrapping her delicate fingers around me and stroking.

My hips jerk forward of their own accord, desire making my balls draw up tight. Suddenly, I'm on the other end of what I was trying to do to Ridge. I was trying to prove a point to him and the others with the way I kissed Sable, and I've got a feeling Trystan is doing the exact same thing.

He wants me to feel her lose control. To feel her come apart from his kiss.

And as her small hand slides up and down my shaft, I have to admit, I don't fuckin' hate it.

If this is sharing, maybe it's not all bad.

With a guttural noise, Sable finally breaks her lips from Trystan's, and Archer is right there. A gentle grip on her chin turns her face toward him, and this time, my wolf doesn't howl in protest as his lips seal over hers.

There's nothing to fucking protest.

The movements of her hand are awkward and a little jerky, making me think she's never done this before, but it doesn't matter. Hell, it makes it better. The sensation of her warm palm and delicate fingers around my cock is the best goddamn thing I've ever felt. There's no shyness or hesitation on her part, nothing but need and desire as she begins to explore Trystan with her other hand, her tongue still tangling with Archer's.

Behind her, Ridge sweeps her hair over one shoulder to give himself access as he tastes the skin of her neck, and I can't help myself. My hand comes up to cup one of her breasts, squeezing and massaging it before rolling her pert nipple between my thumb and forefinger.

Trystan's hand finds the other, and the whimper that pours from Sable's lips is like a chorus of damn angels singing.

Fuck, I want to hear her make that sound over and over.

I want to go to sleep to that sound, wake up to that sound, live and fucking die by that sound.

The fact that the woman of my dreams, the woman my wolf has claimed, is surrounded by three other men who are as dead set on worshipping her body as I am no longer seems quite as strange as it did a few minutes ago. Shifters have never been shy about nudity, so it doesn't bother me to be standing side by side with several other fully naked men.

And honestly, even if I weren't a shifter, I'm not sure I'd even notice or care.

Every bit of my focus is on Sable.

She's the only thing that matters in this equation.

I pinch her nipple lightly again, and she lets out a moan, practically going up on her tiptoes as she kisses Archer harder.

Ridge moves the hand that's splayed over her belly lower, sliding a finger through her folds, and she bucks in our hold, her entire body reacting as if she's channeling an electric current. She arches and undulates against all of us, pressing her breasts into my hand and Trystan's as she grinds against Ridge's finger and kisses Archer like her life depends on it.

The musky, alluring scent of her arousal saturates the air around us, and I'm so damn hard, I swear I'm about to come in her fucking hand.

I'm not the only one who's on edge either.

With a gasp, Sable wrenches her lips away from Archer's. Her cheeks are flushed, her blue eyes glassy, and the silken strands of her blond hair are a mess.

She already looks thoroughly fucked, and we haven't even gotten there yet.

"More!" The word comes out as something between a whimper and a cry. "I need more. I need..."

"We know what you need, little wolf." Ridge's voice is thick with heat.

I catch her gaze, letting the promise ring through my voice. "We've got you."

31

SABLE

WE'VE GOT YOU.

God, I hope that's true. Because I feel like I'm on the verge of floating away, on the precipice of bursting into a million sparks and dissipating in the air.

I have never felt anything like this, not even in the times when I've kissed or touched these men before. This is something altogether different, and I wonder if it's the wolf inside me rising to the surface.

It definitely feels wild, whatever it is. Unrestrained. Uninhibited.

Powerful.

Dare's brown eyes burn as he gazes at me, the flecks of gold in his irises glittering like stars. He looks wild too, masculine and strong, and I can feel his cock pulse against my hand. It's so big I can't even get my fingers all the way around it, but for some reason, that doesn't scare me. It's like my body knows it can take him, knows it was born to fit him.

I've never had sex before. I've barely even gotten to second base before, and if I were with any other men, alarm bells would be ringing in my head, telling me that all of this is too fast, too soon.

There's nothing like that in my mind right now though.

The only mantra running through my head is a single word.

More.

Their hands on me, their mouths on mine, their calloused fingers exploring my body—it's incredible. The most overwhelming thing I've ever experienced.

But it's still not enough.

There's an ache deep in my belly, an emptiness, a yearning. A need for something I can barely articulate but desperately crave.

"Please," I whisper, trying to put everything I'm feeling into that one word. There's no way I manage it—I'm feeling too damn much for an entire novel's worth of words to convey—but I think I get across enough.

Trystan makes a noise low in his throat, and the next thing I know, I'm swept up into his arms, cradled against his chest. I lose my contact with the other men, but it's okay. I can still feel them all around me, and when Trystan turns to stride down the hall toward the bedroom, they're right there with us.

They're not leaving.

None of them.

Just like I asked.

The realization sends a wave of giddy happiness and desire through me, and I cling tighter to Trystan's neck, burying my face in the crook of his shoulder and biting down lightly on the flesh there, tasting the salty warmth of his skin.

"Oh, fuck."

His footsteps falter slightly, and his body goes rigid against mine as he reacts to my touch.

I like it. I like it so much that I bite a little harder, sucking on the skin as if I'm trying to draw out a little piece of his soul.

His breath hitches, a strangled noise resonating in the back of his throat, and he curses again before laying me gently on the bed. His body drapes over mine for a second, and when I finally release his skin with a wet pop, he drops his head and kisses me hard and deep.

It's like he's trying to punish and praise me all at once, and I kiss him back just as desperately, meeting every stroke of his tongue as our teeth bang together. When he finally pulls away, I'm panting for breath again, my lungs struggling to get enough oxygen.

He stands slowly, flanked by the other three as they all gather by the foot of the bed. They're all still naked, so gloriously naked, and I can't stop looking at them. When we arrived at the cabin on that first day and they shifted back to human form with no clothes on, I dragged my gaze away from their nude bodies and ran inside like my hair was on fire.

But that was an old version of Sable. One I'm not even sure exists anymore.

One I sort of hope *won't* exist after tonight.

Instead of shying away, I let my gaze rove everywhere it wants to, soaking up the sight of them and committing it to memory. They're all big men, though Trystan is the tallest of the group, and they're all made of rippling muscle that's highlighted by tan, smooth skin.

And they're all hard.

Their cocks jut out from their bodies, each a slightly different size and shape, and I bite my lip as I study them, doing with my eyes what I did with my hand to Dare earlier—exploring every inch of them.

"Fuck, Sable," Archer murmurs, his normally smooth voice rough with strain. "When you look at us like that..."

There's such open longing in his voice that it makes my chest squeeze, an entirely new kind of ache spreading through me to join the heat already flooding my veins.

I want to keep looking at them. But even more than that, I want to touch.

I want them to touch me.

My skin is still uncomfortably hot, my nerve-endings so sensitive that my clothes feel confining and scratchy. So

I sit up on the bed, reaching down to grab the hem of my shirt before tugging it over my head.

I'm still not wearing a bra, and my nipples tighten as cool air meets my skin. All four of the men standing by the foot of the bed growl, and as I begin to shimmy out of my slightly-too-big jeans, they finally move.

The mattress dips and the bed creaks slightly as they all crawl up beside me. The bed isn't big—it was only built with two occupants in mind, not five—but that just means the men have to crowd closer around me as Dare and Trystan tug the pant legs over my feet before tossing the jeans on the floor.

All that's left is my panties now.

That's the only stitch of clothing anyone in this room is wearing.

And it still feels like way too much.

Dare must think so too, because he grabs them and tears them from my body, flinging them away like they've personally affronted him. The movement is so fast and decisive that it draws a shocked, breathless laugh out of me, and when I look back at his wild features, I find him grinning down at me.

Then his expression grows more serious, and he runs his hands up my legs, his calloused palms gliding over my calves, knees, and thighs. "This is what you want, Sable? Us? This?"

I'm nodding before he's even finished speaking.

There's no reason to hesitate. I've never been more sure of anything in my entire life.

"Yes."

As if that was the single word they've been waiting for, three other sets of hands fall on me too, and my body temperature shoots up as if I've stepped into an inferno. The feral smile reappears on Dare's face as he settles between my legs, gripping my thighs in his large hands to spread them wider apart. I can feel wetness coating my thighs, and all four men must be able to smell my arousal, because suddenly, their caresses border on desperate.

Trystan leans over to kiss me again, picking up where we left off in the living room while Ridge and Archer explore my body with their hands and mouths. And Dare...

I can feel his broad shoulders between my legs, his hold still firm on my thighs. Then I feel the warm tickle of breath on my core, and my entire body tenses with anticipation.

When his warm, wet tongue licks a line all the way up my center, I cry out into Trystan's mouth, my back arching so hard it's like I'm being electrocuted.

"Oh... Oh, God!"

I *feel* the vibrations of the pleased, hungry sound Dare makes, and then he licks me again. Ridge bites down on my nipple at the same time, making sparks explode inside my body.

Archer catches one of my flailing hands, linking our

fingers together to ground me in this storm of sensation even as his own lips trail over the delicate skin of my wrist, awakening nerve-endings I didn't even know existed.

My legs are straining in Dare's grasp, my hips rocking against his face as he licks me, my entire body undulating on the bed as I try to ride out the feelings overpowering me.

This is my first time. I don't know what I'm doing. But then again, I don't *have* to know. These men are so attentive to my every reaction that all I have to do is lie here and *feel*. Let them take care of me.

And they want to. That's obvious in every touch, every kiss.

I let that thought dispel any nerves I might have otherwise, allowing my legs to go pliant in Dare's grip. He gives another satisfied growl low in his throat and spreads my thighs wider, giving himself access to every bit of me.

Trystan draws away from my mouth, but Archer is right there to take his place. My entire body is tingling, burning, humming with sensation, and I've lost track of whose hands are where.

But when the orgasm finally comes crashing over me, I know exactly where Archer's hand is, because I squeeze the shit out of it as a ragged sob tears from my lips, my body shuddering from head to toe.

Dare keeps lapping at me, using the broad, flat part of his tongue, and every lick sends another jolt of pleasure through me. He doesn't let up until I give a little yelp and reach down to push his head away from my sensitized core. He nips at my hand, then grabs it and kisses my palm.

His face is wet. I can feel my own arousal on my skin as he kisses me, and it makes a different kind of heat spread through me. I force my drooping eyelids open to gaze up at the men gathered around me, my chest rising and falling hard as I suck in air.

Ridge's face is the closest to mine, and his amber eyes gleam like fire as his lips curve into a devastating smile. "How do you feel, little wolf?"

"Hungry."

It's not a lie. My body is still shivering from the aftershocks of the orgasm, but I don't feel... complete. I still want something. I still need more.

He chuckles, a low rumble in his chest. "Don't worry. We're not done."

Dare makes a noise of agreement before releasing my hand and crawling up the mattress until his body hovers over mine. He kisses me soundly, and there's a taste I don't recognize on his lips.

Me, I realize with a start. I'm tasting myself.

I groan into his kiss, and he keeps our lips connected as he backs up, pulling me with him until we're both on our knees. The other men shift around us, but I lose track of who's where for a moment as I sink into the depths of Dare's kiss.

Then more hands are on me again, and I'm being lifted, turned... and set down right over Ridge's face.

He's lying on his back. My knees meet the mattress on either side of his head as I straddle him, and for the first time since that indescribable wave of need hit me, a bubble of shyness rises up through my arousal.

I'm... I'm sitting on his face.

The most intimate part of me, the part no man had ever even seen before tonight, is positioned right above his mouth. Dare just had his mouth on me and I didn't feel awkward or embarrassed about that, but this feels different somehow.

Because of the way we're positioned, I can look down and see Ridge's face, poised right at my entrance. And without the mattress at my back, I feel more exposed, more adrift.

Like I'm supposed to be the one in control here.

And *now* I'm worried about my inexperience, about not knowing what to do.

I shift uncomfortably, about to awkwardly clamber off his face, but before I can, he grins up at me.

He looks so... pleased. So hungry.

Just like I'm hungry.

His smile broadens as he loops his arms around my thighs until his fingertips find my core. Then, without an ounce of hesitation, he spreads my folds, baring me even more. And he licks me.

My mouth drops open, my toes curling as my core clenches. It feels like what Dare did, but different too. The way Ridge is holding me open gives him different access to that little bundle of nerves every bit of pleasure radiates from. And my body is still sensitive, still coming down from the previous high, so I swear I can feel each stroke of his tongue *everywhere.*

For a moment, our gazes stay locked. I stare down at him as he works me over with his tongue, and it's one of the dirtiest, sexiest, most beautiful things I've ever seen in my life.

I try to keep my eyes open. I really do. I want to see every bit of this.

But I can't.

As he laps and sucks on me, my eyelids fall shut. His tongue is all over me, wreaking havoc on my body. And then the others are touching me too. Hands are on my breasts, my back, my shoulders, my hair. Lips and teeth and tongues are devouring me.

They're *all* devouring me.

They're going to eat me up.

I groan helplessly, rocking against Ridge's face, grinding against him as need builds inside me again.

A large hand runs down the length of my spine and over the curve of my ass, kneading my flesh before slipping into the space between my cheeks. I jolt when a finger presses against the tight ring of muscles there, and when it slips inside, I clamp my thighs around Ridge's head.

"What... what is...?"

I can't get a full sentence out. All the muscles in my lower body are contracting rhythmically, the foreign invasion and strange feeling of fullness setting off a chain reaction inside me.

"Do you want me to stop?" Trystan's voice is thick, a low murmur near my ear.

"No," I breathe, my heart pounding wildly in my chest.

"Do you want more?"

"Yes," I whimper.

"Fuck."

That's Archer's voice, and he sounds almost as tortured as Trystan does.

As Trystan slides his finger deeper into my ass, I catch hold of Archer's hand again. This time, he brings it to his cock, running my fingertips over the thick length. I'm surprised to find wetness at the tip. I didn't know men got wet from arousal like women did.

I want to explore it. To run my thumb over it, to dip my head and taste it.

But before I can do any of that, Ridge latches on to my core and flicks his tongue back and forth at the same time Trystan slides his finger in another inch.

And I detonate like a bomb.

I thought my first orgasm was overwhelming, but it was

tame compared to this. Dare's lips find mine, and I practically scream into his mouth as I come apart, jerking and writhing and probably half-suffocating Ridge. Not that he seems to mind.

By the time the last wave of pleasure passes, I feel completely boneless. I'm literally not sure I can hold myself up anymore, but I don't have to. Dare and Archer support me as Trystan slowly drags his finger out of my ass, and they lift me off Ridge before depositing me on the bed beside him.

Ridge rolls over and rises to his knees, and once again, I find myself staring up at all four of them.

"Still hungry?" Archer asks, his voice both heated and gentle.

I nod, smiling lazily. Some of the desperation has been burned away, but the deep need is still there.

My core is still clenching, each ripple of my inner walls a reminder of how empty I am. I don't want to be empty. I want to be full.

"Is this your first time, Sable?" Ridge wears a serious expression that lets me know he's already guessed at the answer—hell, they probably all have.

A little flutter of panic fills my stomach. It *is* my first time. I'm a virgin, just like they suspect. But I don't want that to change anything.

I don't want them to stop.

Ridge looks up, meeting the gazes of the other three.

He opens his mouth to speak, but his words come out sounding strange, as if I'm listening to him through a wall of water. I shake my head, trying to clear it.

The fluttering sensation in my belly is growing stronger. Something besides panic. Something besides the heat that overtook me in the living room.

It's like something is growing inside me, expanding outward from the very core of me.

My wolf?

The thought whips through my mind, and suddenly, I'm sure I'm right. It's my wolf. She must've finally been called by the onslaught of extreme emotions, by the attention that's been lavished on me by the four alphas who all claim me as their mate.

I try to say something, but the same muffled sound I heard from Ridge comes out of my mouth too, as if my brain has stopped processing words altogether. But all four men look down at me anyway, drawn by whatever noise I just made.

I expect them to look happy.

My wolf is coming, just like they hoped it would.

I expect them to be pleased.

But as they stare down at me, each one of their faces morphs into a mask of surprise and horror.

Why? I don't understand.

The feeling inside me is expanding faster now. I can

almost feel it pressing against my skin, pushing against the confines of my body. And then...

The scars crisscrossing my body begin to turn a deep, pure black, as if ink is seeping out of my skin and filling in the cracks.

My heart crashes against my ribs as I look down at myself, holding up my arms in horror.

This isn't how the change goes. I've seen these men shift into wolves dozens of times by now, and it never looks like this.

What is happening?

As if the thing inside me is spurred on by my rising panic, dark smoke begins to pour from my fingertips, and the men gathered around me jerk back in surprise.

Dare's chocolate brown eyes meet mine, and for a moment, he just stares at me. Then he opens his mouth, and this time, I *do* hear the words he chokes out. Even if I wish I didn't.

"What the fuck?" He shakes his head, his nostrils flaring as he backs away. "Jesus, Sable. You're not a fucking wolf. You're a witch."

BOOKS BY CALLIE ROSE

Boys of Oak Park Prep
Savage Royals
Defiant Princess
Broken Empire

Kings of Linwood Academy
The Help
The Lie
The Risk

Fallen University
Year One
Year Two
Year Three

Ruthless Games

Sweet Obsession

Sweet Retribution

Sweet Salvation

Made in the USA
Monee, IL
29 October 2020

46369029R00163